THE FACELESS ONES

An organisation which was so mysterious and vast, its people had been called 'The Faceless Ones'; their file, held by the British Security Service, was labelled 'Group X'. So who are these people — what are their intentions? Magda Vettrilli had found out, but before she could pass on her knowledge, she was shot on the steps of the British Consulate in Tangier. Egerton Scott must discover their identity, and the objective behind 'Group X'. But can he succeed?

GERALD VERNER

THE FACELESS ONES

Complete and Unabridged

LINFORD
Leicester

First published in Great Britain

First Linford Edition
published 2013

A catalogue record for this book is available
from the British Library.

ISBN 978–1–4448–1619–8

Published by
F. A. Thorpe (Publishing)
Anstey, Leicestershire

Set by Words & Graphics Ltd.
Anstey, Leicestershire
Printed and bound in Great Britain by
T. J. International Ltd., Padstow, Cornwall

This book is printed on acid-free paper

1

I

Tangier, where anything can happen and usually does, lay under the deep blue of a night sky peppered with brilliant star-points, as though it had been pierced by innumerable pins.

At this hour of the morning, it was nearly half past two, the rue du Statut, the long street that begins at the Grand Socco and winds its way up to the Place de France, was deserted. The noises from the Little Socco, which never sleeps, drifted over the silence, forming a kind of muted background that mingled with the indescribable smells that wafted from the Grand Socco. Against the deep indigo of the sky rose the squat towers of the Kasbah, that ancient Arab stronghold, the gentle waters of the Mediterranean slapping softly at the old stones.

A cold breeze blew whisperingly from

the Straits of Gibraltar, stirring the refuse in the Grand Socco and surging in little fitful gusts up the long incline of the rue Statut. And the street was no longer deserted.

Out of the Place de France came the figure of a woman. She was running, an uneven stumbling run that suggested exhaustion, and staring back over her shoulder every few seconds as though she were afraid of what she might see behind her. She was well dressed, but the expensive fur coat she wore was open and half off one shoulder. Her hair was dishevelled and she carried neither gloves nor handbag. Her face was white and drawn and her eyes wide with fear.

As she ran down the steep hill from the Place de France, her breath coming in great sobbing, erratic gasps, she tried to pull her coat round her shoulder, but there was something which she held tightly clenched in her hand that made this difficult. She managed eventually to pull the coat back on her shoulder and gave a terrified glance up the long street. It stretched away, silent and deserted.

The strained expression on her face relaxed a little. They would follow her, she was in no doubt about that, but she had gained a lead. Would it be long enough to do what she had to do?

She slowed down as she came to the rue du Sud, a turning on the left of the rue du Statut. Further on, on the other side of the street, a broad flight of stone steps led down to the rue Waller. But the rue du Sud would take her to her destination . . .

If she could make it in time!

She turned the corner with another frightened glance up the empty street. As she did so a shivering light flared suddenly on the whitewashed side of a house where the rue du Statut entered the Place de France. It swept along the front of the houses as a car, its headlights blazing turned into the rue du Statut and sped down the hill. It passed the rue du Sud, but the man in the back of the car caught sight of the running woman as she came under a lamp, and shouted to the driver. The car pulled up sharply with a screeching of brakes. The gears ground badly as the driver thrust the lever into reverse.

The woman heard the sound and looked back as the car sped backwards past the end of the street. The terror on her face deepened. Although she was breathless and almost spent, she increased her pace. There was only a short distance to go now . . .

The car reversed again and swung round into the rue du Sud. The headlights picked out the woman's figure as she stumbled round the corner into a side street, and the man in the back seat shouted again to the driver. The car increased its speed. It was nearly level with the woman in the fur coat as she reached the broad steps of a large building and staggered up them. Almost blindly her hand sought and found the bell . . .

But even as her shaking fingers pressed the push, long and urgently, the car slowed. From the window came the sharp, clipped, report of an automatic. Three more shots followed rapidly. The woman gave a convulsive shudder. Her hand dropped from the bell-push as she swayed, fell against the closed door, and crumpled up, like a sawdust doll, on the stone steps.

The car accelerated quickly and sped away into the night . . .

II

At ten o'clock on the following morning the Little Socco baked under the sunglare from a cloudless sky. Amid the heat and the dust a babble of sounds filled the air with noise; the shrill voices of the money changers, the guttural chatter of Arabs in *jalebahs*, in yellow and black striped collarless robes, in modern clothes, crowding and jostling along the narrow street. Donkeys, their bells jangling, walked over the ancient cobblestones, strewn with patches of old and fresh dung, and added to the indescribable clamour.

Making his way through the crowd towards the arch in the wall that leads to the Grand Socco, an elderly man in a crumpled and none too clean white linen suit, a battered panama hat drawn down over his eyes to keep away the glare of the sun, moved with an unhurried step, skilfully avoiding the various knots of people who were swarming around him.

His face was thin and sunburnt to a deep brown, his eyes set in innumerable wrinkles. Across his upper lip straggled a greying moustache. He passed through the arch, crossed the Grand Socco, and mounted the broad steps to the rue Statut. At the entrance to a small shop that sold wine and tobacco, he paused, pushed open the door and entered.

The man behind the counter looked up from opening a parcel of cigarettes.

'Is Mr. Marchment in his room?' asked the newcomer.

The owner of the shop smiled and nodded.

'Yes, Mr. Kettleby,' he answered.

Kettleby grunted. He went over to a door at the back of the shop, opened it, and found himself in a short passage with a narrow staircase that led upward. Ascending the carpetless stairs, he tapped on a door on the right of a small landing.

'Come in,' invited a muffled voice from the room beyond.

Kettleby turned the handle and entered. It was not a very large room and rather poorly furnished. A table occupied the centre of a shabby square of carpet, there was a bookcase against one wall, stuffed with all kinds of books, an easy chair drawn up to an empty grate with a small coffee table beside it, a large cupboard in one corner, and a couple of plain wooden chairs. At the table, in a padded office chair, sat a round-faced, stoutish man with small, beady eyes, who was studying a file of papers that lay open before him.

'Shut the door, Kettleby,' he said, 'and sit down.'

Kettleby shut the door carefully. He took off the panama and threw it on to a chair, revealing a narrow head that was almost completely bald.

'I've heard the news,' he said, pulling the other chair up to the table and sitting down. 'Bad, eh?'

'Very,' replied Marchment, and his beady eyes became even smaller as he drew down the lids. 'I've already notified London.'

He took a cigarette from a box on the table, lit it, and pushed the box towards Kettleby. Kettleby shook his head.

'It's all over Tangier,' he said. 'Magda

must have got on to something pretty serious. Was she able to say anything before she died?'

'Nothing,' answered Marchment. 'She was dead by the time they opened the door at the Consulate. At that hour they were all in bed. They heard the shots and the sound of the car . . . '

'Poor Magda,' said Kettleby. He fingered his straggling moustache. 'She was one of our best agents.'

Marchment nodded. He closed the file in front of him and pushed it away.

'There was nothing on her, I suppose?' said Kettleby.

'Nothing that tells us anything,' replied Marchment. He opened a drawer in the table and took something out. 'They found this — clenched in her left hand.'

He held out a matchbox. Kettleby stretched out his hand and took it. It was an ordinary matchbox. Thousands of a similar kind were on sale throughout Tangier.

'Open it,' said Marchment.

Kettleby did so. In the box were five matches. Two were safety matches, three were of the kind that would strike on anything, with red heads.

Kettleby peered at the matches curiously.

'Magda had this in her hand when she was shot?' he asked.

'Yes. It was so tightly clenched that they had difficulty in opening her fingers.'

'It must mean something,' said Kettleby, frowning.

'Oh yes, it means something,' agreed Marchment. 'But what? There are no markings on the box — nothing to distinguish it from any other box of a similar brand . . . '

'Except the matches,' remarked Kettleby.

'Exactly — except the matches,' said Marchment. 'That's a little unusual, but only Magda knew what it means.'

'And the people who shot her,' muttered Kettleby.

Marchment blew out a stream of tobacco smoke and watched it curl up to the dirty ceiling.

'Group X,' he said softly, and nodded. 'And we know as little about them as we do about the matchbox.'

Kettleby turned the matchbox about in his fingers.

'D'you know what I call 'em?' he asked. 'I call them the 'Faceless Ones.''

Marchment smiled. It was a wry smile that left his small eyes hard.

'Not a bad name, either,' he remarked. 'Pretty well describes them, eh? Faceless, h'm. And bodyless too. *Who* are they, *what* are they, *why* are they?'

'I was never quite sure that they ever existed,' said Kettleby.

'You can be sure now,' retorted Marchment. 'If it's done nothing else, Magda's death has proved *that*. All we had before were rumours that some kind of an organization existed. An incident here, another incident somewhere else. The ravings of a dying man in a German hospital. Nothing concrete, nothing worth a row of pins. But enough to start us wondering. And enough to start the Russians wondering, and the French, and the Chinese. All the various Governments of most of the big countries. Italy, Spain, they contributed a bit. Interpol got hold of several queer facts.'

10

'And Magda discovered something definite,' broke in Kettleby.

'A clever woman,' said Marchment. 'She was given all the information we had and told to bring home the bacon. Well, that's all she brought home — that matchbox! But the fact that she was killed shows that this — call it what you like — Group X — The Faceless Ones — anything you please — is no figment of the imagination. It's real, powerful, and unscrupulous . . .'

'With what object?' interjected Kettleby.

Marchment shrugged his shoulders.

'I don't know,' he answered. 'That's the puzzle. It's not confined to any particular country — it's international. We're not the only people who would like to know 'why'.'

'What's the next move?' asked Kettleby. 'Is there anything you want me to do?'

Marchment shook his head.

'We must wait until we hear from London,' he said. 'They're not on to *us* — yet. At least, I don't think they are.'

'Why do you think that?' asked Kettleby as he picked up his battered panama.

11

'We're still alive, aren't we?' retorted Marchment.

'I see what you mean,' said Kettleby. He walked slowly to the door. 'I'll look in again in the morning,' he said. 'I suppose, I'd better go an' do a little gambling with currency at the money changers, just to keep in character!'

Marchment grinned.

'Don't lose too much,' he said. 'The Department is getting stingy lately.'

When Kettleby had gone, he picked up the matchbox and stared at it thoughtfully for several minutes. Then he got up, went over to the cupboard and unlocked it. In the bottom was a large steel cashbox. He twisted the combination lock until there was a click, opened the heavy lid, put the matchbox inside, and reset the combination.

He went back to the table and lit another cigarette.

III

Sir Edward Fordyce, Director-General of the British Security Service, leaned back in his chair and looked at the man who sat facing him across the big desk.

'That's all I can tell you,' he said.

Egerton Scott's lean face twisted into a grimace.

'There isn't much to go on, is there, sir?' he remarked.

Sir Edward shook his head.

'I'm afraid there isn't,' he replied. 'But it's all we know. As you say, it isn't much. Most of it's the result of patiently piecing together all kinds of apparently unrelated incidents and rumours that have reached us from all over the world. But it all adds up to the fact that there *is* an organization in existence which, for want of a better name, we call 'Group X'.'

'And you believe that this organization has its headquarters in Tangier, sir?' asked Scott.

Sir Edward nodded.

'That's the conclusion we've come to,' he replied. 'Can you think of a better place? Tangier is what is called an international zone: it is ruled by the representatives of many nations. Ideal for an organization of this kind . . . '

'That's just it, sir,' interrupted Egerton Scott. '*What* kind? What's the object? What are they out to *do*?'

'That,' said Sir Edward with a bland smile, 'is what we are very anxious to find out. I believe that Magda Vettrilli *did find out* . . . '

'And that's why she was shot on the steps of the British Consulate?'

'Before she could pass her information on,' finished Sir Edward. 'Yes. These people, whatever their object, are dangerous. Study the précis of all the information we've acquired and you'll see that there's something brewing that's very serious. You've got a copy of the précis among those notes I gave you. When you've studied it, *destroy* it.'

'Anything else?'

'One thing,' Sir Edward shifted in his chair to a more comfortable position. His smooth, rather florid face, under the crisp, greying hair, became very serious. 'This isn't ordinary espionage, you know. There's no Iron Curtain stuff about it. The Russians would like to know what's in the wind as much as we would. So

14

would America and a whole lot of other countries. That means it's dangerous — very dangerous . . . '

Scott smiled.

'I'm used to danger, sir,' he said.

'Not the kind of danger I mean,' answered Sir Edward gravely. 'However, just look after yourself. You can't afford to make a mistake. Now, go and see the Chief of Staff. He's got everything you need, money, passports, the lot!' He rose to his feet and held out his hand across the desk. 'Good luck!'

Egerton Scott rose too. He tucked the slim, leather document case under his left arm and gripped the extended hand.

'Thanks, sir,' he said. 'From what you say I shall need it.'

He shut the door behind him as he came out of the Director-General's office, crossed the outer office, with a nod to Sir Edward's blonde secretary, and went in to the Chief of Staff's room.

The little, bald man behind the littered desk looked up with a smile, and removed the battered pipe from his mouth.

'Finished with the Old Man?' he inquired.

'Yes, I'm in your hands now,' said Scott.

'Good!' The little man glanced at the watch on his wrist. 'We've got twenty minutes before you leave for the airport. There's money in this envelope, and here are your passport and visas. They are in your own name. If you want more money you can get it from Marchment — he's our man in Tangier. Don't try and contact *him*. He'll contact *you*. He'll ask you: 'Is *The Mousetrap* still running in London?' and you'll say: 'It looks like running for ever'. Got that?'

Egerton Scott nodded.

'You're in Tangier on an extended holiday,' the other went on rapidly. 'An uncle of yours has recently died and left you quite a bit of money. You're out for a good time and you thought Tangier was the place to get it. You needn't be too bright, but I don't have to tell you how to play it. There's a room been reserved for you at the Minzeh Hotel. That's about all, I think. You're on your own, now.'

Scott picked up the envelope with the money and the passport and visas.

'What about packing?' he began.

The Chief of Staff grinned.

'It's all been done, my boy,' he said with a wave of his plump hand. 'You'll find all your luggage in the car that's taking you to the airport. If there's anything we've overlooked you can always buy it in Tangier.'

'You seem to have taken care of everything,' said Scott.

'The Department's very thorough,' retorted the other. 'Now, you'd better be off, and the best of British luck to you!'

'I'll send you a postcard,' answered Egerton Scott. 'I believe they have a very special collection in Tangier.'

'You can get anything in Tangier,' said the Chief of Staff, reaching for his pipe.

'Including a bullet in your back,' said Scott.

2

I

The plane from Lisbon circled above the airport at Tangier. The Portuguese steward invited the passengers to fasten their safety belts and put out their cigarettes. He repeated this in a language which he fondly imagined was English. The plane was a small one. It could not be compared to the airliner that had carried Egerton Scott across the Atlantic to New York, or the one from New York to Lisbon.

There were not many passengers. What there were represented several nationalities. The gabble of voices spoke in at least five different languages — it reminded Egerton Scott of an aviary. Among the more silent ones were a well dressed American, an elderly man with grey hair and a rugged face who looked like a prosperous business executive; a thin Chinese of doubtful age, immaculately dressed in an expensive

18

lounge suit that suggested Savile Row; a middle-aged woman in a rather shabby tweed suit, with a long face and gold-rimmed glasses, thin lips and an air of strong disapproval towards everybody. A rather soured spinster was what Scott summed her up as, though he had had no means of verifying this conclusion. But if she wasn't a spinster she ought to be! The rest of the passengers were a mixture of French, Portuguese, Spanish, and Arabs.

The plane, with throttled-back engines, swept down in wider and wider circles. In a few minutes now it would land on the runway . . .

And then, thought Egerton, the assignment would begin . . .

Yes, but where? How?

During his overnight stay in New York he had read and re-read the notes given to him by Sir Edward Fordyce. They were vague and on the surface unrelated, but they definitely added up to something. You could trace an attenuated thread that linked them together. One of the top American scientists, a physicist whose discoveries in nuclear fission had been outstanding, had been blown to pieces in his laboratory. The explosion was at first supposed to be the result of an experiment that had gone wrong. But among the debris the experts had found traces of a bomb with portions of a time-fuse. The scientist and his two assistants, together with the notes of a number of new ideas on which they had been working, had been destroyed. Two Russian scientists had disappeared completely. A number of cases of sabotage in various rocket stations and atomic power plants had taken place in several countries. In Western Germany, a man had been surprised in an attempt to set fire to the house of a leading chemist. He had been shot while trying to make his escape. Before he died in the hospital to which he had been taken, he had raved in delirium, disjointed words trailing away into unintelligible mutterings about security, destruction, and the new world that was coming. In England there had been innumerable cases of attempts to stir up demonstrations against the use of nuclear weapons. In every instance it had been impossible to trace the originators. There were hundreds of these apparently isolated incidents, gathered from all corners of the world over a period of three years, that clearly showed that there was some definite organization behind them. A powerful group with branches in nearly every civilized country, controlled by, possibly, one head branch from which the orders were issued.

What was the object? thought Egerton Scott, as the plane began its final circle of the airport before touching down. Was it just a case of trying to foment trouble? Or was there some commercial angle — Big Business with two capital B's? Or was it merely fanatical? Certainly it used fanatics, but, then, fanatics had been used before by hard, clear thinking men for their own ends.

It was difficult to come to any real conclusion. There was so little data. But it was going to be a tricky business — and dangerous . . .

The wheels of the plane bumped gently on the runway. It bounced a little, steadied, and ran over the tarmac to come to a halt opposite the entrance to the airport station.

The passengers crowded to the door, and Egerton Scott followed more slowly. As he, presently, came down the stairway from the plane, a warm sun greeted him. Tangier airport is built in mountain country above and behind the city itself which is nearly seven miles away.

As Egerton made his way to the Customs and to have his passport stamped, he hoped that the hotel people had sent the car to meet him which he had ordered by telegram from Lisbon.

He had no difficulty with the Customs. All the notes given him by Sir Edward he had destroyed in New York, and there was nothing that was likely to delay him passing through. He found himself on a wide, rather rocky, open space in which several cars were standing. The American business man followed him out and eyed the waiting cars keenly.

'I guess, one of these cars must be from the hotel,' he remarked to the muscular Arab who was handling his luggage. 'Now, which would it be?'

The Arab smiled brightly and pointed a brown finger. A short, stoutish driver in uniform detached himself from the side of a car with a shooting brake body and came over.

'It is for the Minzeh Hotel you wish, m'sieu'?' he said.

'That's so,' agreed the American.

'There is another for which I wait . . . ' began the driver.

'That's me,' interrupted Scott, beckoning to the other Arab porter to hurry with his luggage. 'I'm staying at the Minzeh.'

'I guess we're fellow-travellers, sir,' said the American, his rugged face lighting up with a wide smile that revealed a set of teeth that had never been devised by nature. 'My name is John P. Ogden. Pleased to know you.'

He held out a large but well-shaped hand and gave Scott a hearty grip.

'Mine's Scott — Egerton Scott,' said Scott.

The Arab porters stowed the luggage in the hotel brake and were suitably tipped. The driver got up behind the wheel, and Scott and Ogden settled themselves in the seat behind him. He scarcely waited for them to sit down before he sent the car shooting down the mountain road like a rocket. At the slight bend another car was coming towards them and, without taking his foot off the accelerator, the driver flicked the wheel, pressed on the button of the horn, and shaved past the other car with scarcely an inch to spare.

'That was pretty near,' said Scott.

John P. Ogden chuckled.

'This is your first visit to Tangier?' he asked.

'Yes,' answered Scott.

'I guess, you'll get used to the driving,' said the American. 'They all drive like this. Just keep the horn going and hope for the best.'

'Many accidents?'

'Not as many as you'd think. I'll say it's a bit nerve racking until you get used to it.'

Egerton thought it might take him some time to get acclimatized. He said:

'This isn't your first visit, I gather?'

The other shook his head.

'No, sir,' he replied. 'I come over about three times each year. Got business interests. Are you here on business?'

'Holiday,' said Scott. 'I've heard you can have a good time without too many restrictions.'

'I guess, that's true. There aren't many restrictions in Tangier. Maybe, I can show you around. How long are you figuring on staying?'

'That depends on what sort of a time I'm having,' answered Scott with a grin.

'You won't have any complaints,' retorted Ogden. 'If there's anything you can't get, or do, in Tangier, I guess I've never heard of it.'

He began to enumerate some of the attractions that Tangier had to offer and was still in the middle of his semi-humorous catalogue when they arrived at their destination.

At the reception desk they parted company with a rather vague arrange-ment to meet in the bar later, and Scott was taken up to his room. After he had unpacked he had a hot bath, put on a fresh suit, and decided to explore a part of Tangier. He strolled down the rue Statut to the steps leading down to the

Grand Socco. A babel of noise greeted his ears and a profusion of smells assailed his flinching nostrils. Crowds of people of all ages and nationalities were jostling each other, shouting and gesticulating, and, apparently, without any idea as to where they were going. The bells of the donkeys and the cries of their owners added to the din. Scott was fascinated. It reminded him of Petticoat Lane except that it was more colourful. The red tarboosh was everywhere. Arabs in *jalebahs* moved with stately slowness. In the earthen market there were masses of flowers of all kinds and great piles of fruit. There were several smartly dressed French women among the crowd, a few Americans with cameras on leathern straps, English and Danish sailors, groups of Frenchmen, jabbering excitedly to each other, a smattering of Spanish, and Portuguese of both sexes — a cosmopolitan gathering that represented the four corners of the earth.

Egerton Scott threaded his way slowly through the throng until he came to the arch that led into the Little Socco. The noise was even louder and more raucous and the smells more pungent. As he passed under the arch, a man in a soiled white linen suit and a panama hat bumped into him. He apologized rather ungraciously and went on into the Grand Socco.

An Englishman run to seed, thought Scott. As so many did who stayed out East for any length of time. He strolled about for some time, watching the different stratas of humanity milling around him, and then feeling a little tired, he made his way back to the hotel.

Putting his hand in his jacket pocket for his lighter he pulled out with it a scrap of paper. It was crumpled, and he straightened it out. There was a message scrawled in pencil: '*Be in the Flamenco Bar at ten-thirty.*'

That was all but it was enough. The 'contact' had wasted no time in getting in touch with him.

II

After an excellent dinner in the hotel, which occupied him until nearly nine o'clock, and a couple of drinks in the well-appointed bar with his new acquaintance John P. Ogden, Egerton Scott made an excuse to the American, who was all for taking him on a sightseeing tour of Tangier, and set out to find the Flamenco Bar.

It was a fine night. The sky was a soft and very deep blue, like an arch of velvet, in which the stars hung with the brilliance of diamonds in a show case. Scott had no idea of the whereabouts of the Flamenco — he had preferred not to inquire at the Minzeh — but he secured the required information from an American sailor.

'About half-way along on the right of the rue San Francisco,' said the sailor, looking at him a trifle peculiarly. 'It runs along by the Grand Socco, a narrow hill. You been to the Flamenco before, bud?'

Egerton Scott shook his head.

'I guess, it's a bum sort o' joint,' remarked the sailor. 'The Parade's the best bar . . . '

'I've got to meet a friend,' explained Scott.

'Okay, buddy,' replied the sailor. 'But keep yer hand on your wallet!'

'Like that, eh?'

'An' then some!' The big sailor grinned. He shifted a wad of gum from one side of his mouth to the other. 'Enjoy your evenin',' he said and walked quickly away.

Egerton Scott went in search of the rue San Francisco with mixed feelings. The Flamenco sounded as if it might be interesting.

A neon sign in green gleamed brightly over the entrance to the bar in the narrow street. Two cars roared down the hill with their horns screaming as he pushed open the door and went in.

The bar was not very big and was painted in garish colours with a great deal of chromium. Along one side, under a mural that was so blatantly vulgar, and so atrociously painted, that it offended the sight, ran a padded seat with several small tables in front of it. There were padded stools in front of the bar that stretched across the opposite side of the long, but rather narrow, room. At the end facing the entrance, curtains draped an archway. Strip lighting in red, blue, and white glared down from the ceiling.

The place was pretty full. The padded seat was wedged tightly with people of various nationalities and sexes. There was a babble of voices, speaking in several languages, and the place was full of tobacco smoke in spite of the fan extractor that was spinning in the wall beside the door.

Behind the bar, one wiping glasses and the other opening a bottle of gin, were two swarthy Spaniards in coats that had once been white.

Scott went up to the bar, edged his way between the broad back of a stout Frenchman who was gabbling away to a bored-looking girl, and the thinner back of a bearded German, and ordered a double Haig. There was no cessation in the babble of voices, but he sensed that his entrance had been noticed and marked by everybody in the bar.

And the atmosphere was definitely hostile. He was a stranger and his presence was resented.

The Spaniard who was wiping the glasses put down the cloth he was using and served him. His face was unsmiling.

Scott paid for the whisky and helped himself to a little water from the jug on the counter.

He wondered, as he drank, why such a place had been chosen for him to meet his contact. Surely there must be some better, a more suitable, rendezvous?

He looked at his watch. It was nearly half past ten. Was the man he was expecting already here? He looked round casually at the mixed crowd. The man would, of course, approach him . . .

The door opened and a man in a soiled white linen suit and a battered panama hat came in. And there was no doubt that he was a little drunk. He staggered slightly as he made his way to the bar, and ordered a double rum.

That he was a well-known habitué of the place was evident. Several people greeted him with friendly remarks, and the dark-featured Spaniards allowed their hard faces to relax into smiles.

He threw some coins down to pay for his rum, picked up the glass, and as he did so staggered into Scott. To balance himself he clutched at Scott's arm. There was a general chuckle and the Spanish barmen winked at each other.

'I — I'm sho shorry,' apologized the newcomer, swaying slightly. 'Very s-shorry.'

'That's all right,' said Scott. 'Look out, you're spilling your drink.'

'Mustn't do that,' said the other. He straightened the glass, raised it to his lips and gulped down the contents. 'Tha's better . . . I say, you — you're English, eh?'

Scott agreed that he was.

'I — I'm English, too. Name's Kettleby, Wawas' yours?'

'Scott — Egerton Scott . . . '

'Always glad to meet a fellow Englishman,' said Kettleby. 'Long time since I was in England — long time.' He shook his head mournfully. 'Too long! How's dear ol' Lunnon, eh?'

'Much the same as ever,' said Scott.

'Is *The Mousetrap* still running?' asked Kettleby.

'It looks like running for ever,' answered Scott.

This was it. This was the arranged recognition. But he was puzzled. This man's name was Kettleby. He had been told that the contact was somebody named Marchment.

'Jol — jolly good show,' went on Kettleby with difficulty. 'Last show I saw be — before I left Lon'on. Les' have another drink. What you drinking?' He turned to the bar.

''Nother double rum,' he ordered, 'an' whatever this gen'l'man's drinking.'

A double Haig was pushed towards Scott. Kettleby fumbled through the pockets of his crumpled suit and found a crumpled note. He dropped it on the bar and took the rum which the barman held out to him in shaking fingers. He drank a little of it, put it down on the bar, took out a none too clean handkerchief and mopped his face.

'Ver' — ver' shtuffy in here,' he said unsteadily. 'Mus' get some air.'

He made a movement to pick up his drink and knocked the glass over. The rum ran all over the bar and he looked at it stupidly.

'C-clumsy,' he muttered. 'Waste of g-good rum.'

Scott winked at the barman as the man mopped up the pool of spirit.

Kettleby hiccuped. 'Better get some fresh air,' he muttered thickly. 'Not f-feeling too good . . .'

'Which way are you going?' asked Scott.

The other made a vague gesture.

'D-down street,' he said, swaying like a sapling in the wind. 'B-b-better be getting along . . .'

He turned towards the door, stumbled and clutched at a stool to save himself from falling.

Egerton Scott drank his whisky.

'I'm going that way,' he said. 'I'll set you on your way.'

'Tha's ver' kind of you,' said Kettleby. 'F-feel a b-bit under the weather . . .'

Scott took his arm and steered his wavering steps to the entrance. As they went out a shout of laughter followed them. Kettleby was still staggering drunkenly as they moved off down the rue San Francisco, but his voice, when he spoke, was firm and steady.

'Got the reputation of being a bit of a

soak,' he said in a low voice. 'Useful. Nobody bothers about me, you see.'

Scott nodded. 'What do we do now?' he asked.

'You leave me at the end of the street,' replied Kettleby. 'Just as I stagger away a car will draw up beside you. Hop in. Marchment will be driving.'

'Very neat,' said Scott.

'Don't think anyone suspects that I'm anything but a rather down-at-heel drunk living on a remittance from home,' remarked the other. 'I make a bit on the side by playing the currency. It's a hell of a life!' He sighed. 'This is where we part company for the time being. I expect I'll be seeing you again some time.'

They had reached the end of the rue San Francisco and Kettleby with a slurred and incoherent, but effusive, farewell, staggered away uncertainly in the direction of the Little Socco. Almost at once a car with its horn screaming, and driven with that reckless disregard for life and limb which is a feature of Tangier, came tearing down the narrow street and drew up beside Egerton Scott.

It was a rather ancient Ford. The man behind the wheel leaned forward and opened the door. Scott doubled himself up and slid into the car, pulling the door shut. It started off again at once. He glanced at the thick-set figure of the driver.

'I'm Marchment,' remarked the man at the wheel. 'Sorry about the car. Terrible old crock, but it still goes! I'm not supposed to have much money, so I can't run to anything better. What d'you think of Tangier, eh?'

'I haven't seen much of it yet,' answered Scott.

'No, I suppose not,' said Marchment. 'It has its points and it has other things as well! We'll drive along the Old Mountain Road. We can talk over things as we go along. There's nothing like a car for privacy. No risk of being overheard, eh?'

Scott agreed.

'I expect they've given you all the gen?' went on Marchment. 'What there is of it.'

'What there is of it is the operative phrase,' said Scott. 'It's all very much conjecture, isn't it? You can only deduce that some kind of an organization exists somewhere. There's no definite proof . . . '

'Except the killing of Magda,' broke in Marchment. 'That rather pin-points it. She found out something that would have been proof. Don't run away with the idea that we've all got bees in our bonnets over this, Scott. It's *real*. There's a vast organization that has been built up over a period of years, with ramifications all over the world. Every country has its own unit, but the orders come from a central headquarters . . . '

'Which you believe is here — in Tangier,' broke in Scott. 'Why?'

'Again because of what happened to Magda,' said Marchment. 'That's what she was here for. And she was shot . . . '

'But what's the object of this organization?' demanded Egerton Scott. 'What are they out to do?'

'I wish I could tell you,' said Marchment. 'That's what you're here for — to take over where poor Magda left off.'

'Nice easy sort of job I've got, haven't I?' said Scott bitterly. 'Like looking for a needle in a haystack. All there is to go on is a matchbox . . . '

'With two safety matches and three red-headed matches,' finished Marchment. 'It means quite a lot — if we could understand it.'

'You're sure there's no message concealed in it?'

Marchment shook his head. They were running along a twisting road lined with trees. The lights of one or two houses, standing back from the road at unequal distances, shone through the thick foliage, and there were several more scattered up the wooded hillside.

'There's nothing,' he said. 'It's just an ordinary matchbox. That was the first thing I expected, of course. But there's nothing. I've gone over it again and again . . . '

'Well, that doesn't seem to help us at the moment,' said Scott. 'Where did Magda live?'

'26-bis Marshan,' answered the other. 'She had a flat in a block. Marshan is a huge, flat, open space, very select. But there's nothing in her flat to help us. It had been ransacked, and anything that might have been there, removed. These people are very thorough.'

'Friends?' suggested Egerton.

'You might be luckier there,' answered Marchment. 'But you'll have to go very cautiously. If it gets around that you are making inquiries about Magda . . . ' He shrugged his broad shoulders.

'Bullets in the back, I suppose?' grunted Scott.

'Or something equally nasty,' said Marchment. 'She used to go quite frequently to a club called The Cosmo. It's highly respectable. Dancing, good food, the finest wines. You might get on to something there.'

'What about the police? I suppose there are police in this queer place?'

Marchment chuckled.

'Oh yes,' he replied. 'Very efficient too. They are controlled by the Belgians. The French control the Customs. You see, Tangier is ruled by the representatives of many nations. The police, of course, are investigating the murder. But *we* can't work with them. That's the difficulty. *We don't know who may belong to this organization.*'

'I see,' muttered Egerton Scott.

'The people running this show, whatever it is,' said Marchment seriously, 'are Big with a capital B. And the funds behind them must be enormous. Whatever they are out to do is nothing petty. It's something so big that it justifies any means to attain its object . . . '

'It'ud make it easier if we knew what that was,' interrupted Scott. 'What's your opinion?'

'I don't know,' declared Marchment. 'It's not easy. I don't think it's political — certainly it isn't anything to do with Communism. It could be for gain . . . '

'A criminal organization, you mean?' said Scott.

'Something of the sort,' admitted Marchment. 'If it is, it's on a huge scale and the visualized gain must be astronomical. It's not much good speculating.'

'Well,' remarked Scott grimly, 'I've had several difficult assignments from the Department, but this looks like being the toughest.'

'I'm not contradicting you,' retorted Marchment. 'Maybe you'll crack it. Let's hope so. It will be better if you and I and

Kettleby keep well out of each others way in future. Kettleby and I are known to be old friends — two failures who've gravitated together in a foreign country — but you'd better not get mixed up with us. You'll need some means of getting about. What about getting yourself a car?'

'I might do that,' said Scott.

'I should. I'll tell you why. We must keep in touch. You may need help and you'll want money. There's an isolated ruin called the Hassan Tower on the outskirts of Rabat. Rabat is quite a good way from Tangier but you could get there pretty easily by car. We could always meet at the Hassan Tower without any danger of being seen.'

'How do I get in touch with you to make the appointment?' asked Scott.

'There's a café in the Little Socco with a yellow awning over the front,' answered Marchment. 'Kettleby will be having coffee there every morning from ten until a quarter past. You don't have to speak to him. Just order a coffee and I shall know that you will be at the Hassan Tower that afternoon round about four o'clock.'

It was late when Scott got back to the Minzeh Hotel. Marchment had dropped him at the lower part of the rue Statut, and he had walked up the long street. He felt very tired and quite ready for bed. But he wasn't too tired to notice that his things were not *quite* as he had left them.

His room had been expertly searched, but not expertly enough to deceive an old hand at the game like himself!

3

I

Egerton Scott undressed slowly. He had a hot bath, put on a dressing gown over his pyjamas, poured himself out a whisky from the bottle of Haig which he had ordered to be sent up to his room, and sat down to think.

The searching of his room was a little disconcerting. Did these people suspect that he was not what he appeared on the surface, or was it just a routine precaution that was carried out on new arrivals? They had certainly found nothing among his belongings to justify any suspicions that they might have had concerning him. Everything that he had was in character. There was nothing to even remotely suggest that he was other than he seemed.

But it was worrying all the same.

It suggested a thoroughness that was not a little frightening.

He lit a cigarette and started to make his plans for the following day. The Cosmo Club seemed the proper place to make a start. Magda had spent quite a lot of her time there, according to Marchment, and it was there that she might have stumbled on the clue that had led to her death.

A box of ordinary matches?

What possible significance did it have? A box of matches containing two safety and three matches that would strike on anything . . .

Marchment had said that there was nothing about the box itself that was at all unusual. So the secret must be in the matches.

Scott puzzled his brains for a long time, but he failed to reach any reasonable conclusion, and at last he went to bed, to sleep dreamlessly until he was awakened by the arrival of his morning tea.

II

The Cosmo Club was a pretentious building situated in the Place de France.

It consisted of a dining room, a small dance floor which opened off the dining room, a lounge that was extremely comfortable, with an excellently appointed bar. Beyond the lounge was a card room and, beyond that again, a large room where there was a roulette wheel. The decoration was gay but in the best possible taste; the lighting subdued but adequate, and all the appointments were of the most expensive.

A guitarist band played discreetly on a raised dais in the dining room, and a small dance band provided the necessary accompaniment for dancing.

The Cosmo was definitely a membership club. Unless you were a member, or the guest of a member, there was no admittance to these exclusive amenities, and it was due to his American acquaintance, John P. Ogden, that Egerton Scott found himself seated at an exquisitely laid table in the dining room that evening, listening to the strains of Enrico Silvo's Guitarist Band and enjoying one of the best dinners he had ever tasted.

He had mentioned the Cosmo to the

receptionist at the hotel and had been overheard by Mr. Ogden, who had waxed volubly enthusiastic on the subject.

'Say, that's one of the places I was going to introduce you to, Scott,' he said. 'I've been all over this little world an' there's nothing better in any country. I'd be glad for you to be my guest for dinner this evening . . . '

'You be mine,' said Scott, and it was then that he learned that only members were allowed.

'I guess I can fix you up for membership, later,' said Ogden, 'but it takes a day or two. It's not one of those places you can pay a subscription an' become a member at once. No sir! Manuel keeps it strictly exclusive . . . '

Scott had been introduced to Manuel Mendoza, the manager of the Cosmo Club, a slim, good-looking Spaniard with snaky hips and a calculating eye, who had agreed to facilitate Egerton Scott's membership. He spoke almost faultless English and Scott learned later that he could speak French, Italian, German and Portuguese with equal fluency.

The dining room was fairly full with, what Scott concluded, were the élite of Tangier. At least they all looked very prosperous which, considering the prices, was an extremely necessary adjunct of membership. Nearly every nationality was represented, a cosmopolitan gathering with only one common denominator — money.

There was a long table at one end of the room which had been laid for dinner but was still vacant. A profusion of flowers, crystal glass, silver, and white napery had been arranged with care and artistry. Gold-topped bottles rested in nests of ice in champagne coolers at either end of the table, and the head waiter hovered round anxiously, like a hen over a newly hatched chick, to ensure that everything was as it should be.

Egerton Scott drew his American host's attention to this vacant table.

'I wonder who the party is for?' he said.

John P. Ogden shook his head.

'I wouldn't know,' he replied. 'Some anniversary, or birthday, party, I guess.'

The manager came in at that moment

and joined the head waiter. He looked over the arrangements of the table, made some remarks concerning the position of a vase of flowers, and nodded approvingly when it had been changed. On his way out he paused at their table with a smile that showed his even white teeth.

'Everything is all right?' he inquired.

'Fine!' answered the American. 'Say, whose party is the table for?'

'Mrs. Alison Mae Swanson,' said Manuel, lowering his voice to a hushed deference. 'She is bringing a party from her yacht this evening.'

The name struck a chord in Scott's memory but he couldn't recall in what connection. To John P. Ogden, however, it obviously meant a great deal. His lips pursed in a silent whistle.

'Alison Mae Swanson, eh?' he repeated.

'She always dines here when her yacht is anchored in the bay,' said Manuel. 'It is a great honour. We always do our very best.'

He moved away to another table, and Scott raised an inquiring eyebrow.

'Who is this woman?' he asked. 'I seem

48

to know the name . . . '

'She's the richest woman in the world!' said Mr. Ogden. 'Yes, sir! I guess she's got more dollars than the President! That gal was the sole heiress to old A. D. Chalkpenny . . . '

'Chalkpenny's Hamburgers,' broke in Scott. 'I remember now. She married Swanson three years ago and divorced him in six months.'

Ogden opened his mouth to reply and shut it again as a sudden buzz of interest circulated round the dining room. Preceded by a very deferential Manuel Mendoza, the head waiter, and a small army of minor waiters, all in slavish abasement, a tall, slim, and elegant woman, glittering with diamonds, and dressed in a white gown, the apparent simplicity of which denoted its extreme expensiveness, entered the dining room and was ushered with great obsequiousness to a seat at the head of the long table. In her train followed five men and five women none of whom, however, equalled, either in appearance or appurtenance, their regal hostess.

Egerton Scott watched the party settle down at the table with interest. Alison Mae Swanson was not beautiful. She was not even pretty. But there was something about her that was almost magnetic. He tried to find a word that would describe her attractiveness and failed. The nearest he could get was 'personality.' Her guests were less distinguished. The men were a mixed bunch. Two of them were definitely agéd, and the other three long past their prime. The women were younger, but none of them was particularly attractive.

A low chuckle from his host turned Scott's attention back to Mr. Ogden.

'I guess, dollars attract dollars,' he remarked. 'I don't know about the others, but at least two of those guys are multi-millionaires.'

'You know them?' asked Scott.

Mr. Ogden shook his head.

'No, sir. I can't claim to have an acquaintance with such rare fish. But I know of them. That guy with the grey hair, the tall one, is Robert H. Glenn, the American steel man. The short, stout feller, with the little beard is Montague

Richards, the banker. Say, you ought to know him, he's a Britisher.'

He took a sip of his wine.

'If the others are only half as rich,' he went on with a broad smile, 'the combined resources of that table 'ud pay a couple of national debts and still leave enough over for the children's pocket money!'

'I wonder who the others are,' murmured Scott.

'My information has run dry,' said John P. Ogden. 'They're foreigners from the look of 'em. You'll take brandy with your coffee?'

Scott assented and was glad he had. It was a good brandy, and so was the cigar that he chose from the trolley. The entire dinner had been excellent. He doubted if the cooking, the wines, or the service could have been surpassed anywhere in the world.

Mr. Ogden was obviously pleased when he said so.

'I guess, a meal like that kinda makes you feel at peace with the world,' he remarked. 'Manuel surely knows his stuff.

By the way,' he leaned across the table, 'have you heard about this woman who was murdered? Shot on the steps of your Consulate the other night.'

'I heard something about it,' answered Scott. 'Who was she?'

'A woman called Magda Something-or-other,' answered the American, cupping the bowl of his brandy glass in his two hands. 'Mysterious kinda business from what I can hear. I reckon there's politics at the root of it.'

'Who shot her?' inquired Scott.

Mr. Ogden shook his head.

'Nobody seems to know,' he said. 'The shots were fired from a car. I guess that may be all poppycock! Maybe they know well enough, but don't want to say so.'

'What makes you so interested?' asked Scott.

'I'm a keen student of crime,' answered the other. 'These kinda things get me interested. Queer things happen in this part of the world. Say, the party's not what you'd call a wow, is it?'

The party appeared to Egerton Scott to be very dull. The woman at the head of the table was silent, and the rest of them seemed to be concentrating on the food set before them.

'Not by any means riotous,' he replied. 'I suppose, when you've all that money it gets you like that.'

'It wouldn't get *me* like that,' declared Mr. Ogden. 'No, sir! I guess, I could still put on a broad smile while the millions piled up!'

At his suggestion they went into the bar. It was nearly empty. One or two people were drinking cocktails at the small tables, and the manager, Manuel Mendoza, appeared to be having an argument with a woman at the bar itself. She was the elderly spinster who had been on the plane.

'But, my good man,' she was saying in a high, harsh, strident voice. 'You don't seem to understand. I am Lady Boynton-Smith! I wish to dine here . . . '

'Madam,' answered Manuel politely. 'I explain to you. Only members are admitted . . . '

'That's absolute rubbish,' interrupted Lady Boynton-Smith.

'Do you not, madam,' said the patient Manuel, 'have clubs in England that are only for members?'

'That is quite a different thing,' retorted Lady Boynton-Smith. 'This is *not* England.'

'No, madam,' said the manager, 'but at the Cosmo the same rules apply. I regret so very much at having to refuse you . . .'

'I shall take the matter up with the Consul,' declared Lady Boynton-Smith. 'I think it is disgraceful!' Her long, rather horse-like face was slightly flushed with indignation as she surveyed Manuel haughtily through her gold-rimmed glasses. 'There should be some kind of preferential treatment for distinguished visitors . . .'

'Ah, but then how could one keep the place select, madam?' asked Manuel, spreading his hands. 'If one allowed all the tourists to come in who arrived in Tangier . . .'

'I quite agree that that would be impossible,' said Lady Boynton-Smith. 'But there are exceptions. In *my* case . . .'

'If one makes one exception, then one has to make others. It is like the snowball rolling down the hillside. It becomes bigger and bigger until it gets unwieldy. You understand?'

Lady Boynton-Smith's thin lips compressed until they almost vanished altogether.

'I take it, then,' she said icily, 'that you will not allow me to dine here?'

'I am desolated to have to refuse madam,' said the manager regretfully, 'but . . . ' He hunched up his shoulders in an expressive gesture.

Lady Boynton-Smith gave him a look such as she might have bestowed on something that had crawled out from under a stone in her garden. Without another word she turned and stalked haughtily out.

The manager looked round, saw Scott and the American had been interested spectators of the scene, and smiled ruefully.

'That one is what you call a Tartar,' he said.

'The type of Britisher that always gets my goat,' declared Mr. Ogden. 'Imagines that the world was made entirely for their pleasure. Have a drink, Manuel?'

Egerton Scott said nothing. He happened to know Lady Boynton-Smith, and, if there was one thing more certain than another, it was that the woman who had just left the Cosmo Club was not she!

III

Egerton Scott sat in the big easy chair in his bedroom at the hotel and smoked thoughtfully. It was a little after eleven o'clock. John P. Ogden had wanted to make a night of it, suggesting a varied assortment of amusements that could be obtained in Tangier, but Scott had pleaded a headache. They had therefore, reluctantly on the part of Mr. Ogden, returned to the Minzeh.

The headache was in a sense real, but it was more mental than physical. This assignment was going to be more difficult than he had anticipated. There was no jumping off place. The obvious start was Magda, and he couldn't go around questioning people about her without drawing unwelcome attention to himself. She must have had friends in Tangier — possibly at the Cosmo Club. But how was he to distinguish who might have been her real friends and who her enemies?

He had brought the subject of Magda's murder up in the bar, casually as though making conversation, while he and the American had been drinking with Manuel Mendoza. And Manuel Mendoza had suddenly been called away. At least that's the excuse he offered for not discussing the matter.

Quite possibly there was nothing more in Mendoza's reluctance to talk about a member of the club than the fact that the manner of her death had been so sensational. It was not the kind of thing that the select habitués of the establishment would wish to be mixed up with.

On the other hand there could be another reason. Mendoza might know a great deal more about it than he wanted known.

Of course, the police must have made exhaustive enquiries. The rational thing would be to disclose his identity to the official in charge of the murder and get all the gen from him. But that was too risky. You couldn't tell who was mixed up in this organization. It was so large and widespread that the most unexpected people might be attached to it.

No, he had to work under cover.

He lit another cigarette and settled himself more comfortably in his chair. When Magda had sought refuge at the British Consulate that night, where had she come from? From the Cosmo Club? Was it there that she had discovered whatever it was that she *had* discovered?

Scott flicked the ash from his cigarette on to the carpet irritably. It was all so vague. All so much in the air. Nobody knew what it was that she had found out . . .

A matchbox!

Something stirred in the deep recesses of his mind — way down below the conscious. Something to do with that matchbox. Vainly he tried to pin down the elusive thing but it refused to take either shape or coherence. It was just an unease. Perhaps, if he left it alone, it would swim up into his conscious mind, clear and complete . . .

What about the woman who had called

herself 'Lady Boynton-Smith'? Was that just to impress, or was there more to it? Was she part and parcel of this queer set-up?

Scott smiled as he pictured the real Lady Boynton-Smith, who happened to be the aunt of one of his friends. A sweet old lady with white hair who would never dream of behaving as this other woman had. It was pure coincidence that he should have known her — one of those coincidences that happen so often. He hadn't said anything to Mendoza or Ogden. The knowledge was better kept to himself. You never knew how useful it might turn out . . .

The thing he had to decide was what course of action he was going to take in this business. It was no good just sitting around, he would have to *make* something happen. When people got a severe jolt they sometimes did silly things. But it was difficult to administer this kind of treatment unless you knew *who* to administer it to . . .

He lit his seventh cigarette.

IV

Sir Edward Fordyce frowned down at the decoded dispatch which lay on his desk. He stretched out his hand and flicked the switch of the intercom.

'Ask the Chief of Staff to come and see me,' he said to his secretary.

After a few seconds the Chief of Staff came in.

'Sit down,' said Sir Edward, nodding towards the chair that faced him across the big desk. 'There have been three more alleged suicides. One in Russia, two in America.'

The little, bald man pursed his lips.

'Nuclear scientists?' he inquired.

Sir Edward nodded. His long fingers caressed his chin.

'Yes,' he replied. 'That makes fourteen altogether. All during the past eighteen months.'

'And nothing to show that they weren't genuine suicides?' remarked the Chief of Staff.

'Nothing.' Sir Edward shook his head. 'But — well, fourteen suicides among top men is a bit too much to swallow, don't you think?'

'You're suggesting that they were murdered, sir?' asked the Chief of Staff.

'Yes. Very cleverly, of course. They all shot themselves, and the gun was found either in their hand or nearby. No other fingerprints were found on it. That was invariable in every case. Suspicious, eh?'

'More than suspicious, sir,' answered the little man. 'It's inconceivable to imagine that all these people would have chosen the same method. And the deaths were widespread. We had two in this country.'

Sir Edward reached out and took a cigarette from the box on his desk. Deliberately, he flicked a lighter into flame and dipped the end of the cigarette in it.

'That's not all,' he said, blowing out a thin stream of smoke and leaning back in his chair. 'An explosion has wrecked one of the principal rocket factories in Russia, and two nuclear submarines have been seriously damaged in America. The matter is being hushed up, but the news came this morning.' He patted the dispatch in front of him. 'If you add up all these apparently isolated incidents, the total doesn't leave much room for doubt, eh?'

'An organized group,' said the Chief of Staff. 'In fact 'Group X'.'

'Group X,' repeated Sir Edward. 'I suppose there has been no message from Scott?'

'There's hardly been time, sir,' said the Chief of Staff. He put his hand in his pocket and brought out his battered pipe. Polishing the bowl on the palm of his hand, he frowned. 'What's the idea?' he went on. 'What's the object behind this — I don't know what to call it — murder, sabotage? . . . '

'Whatever it is it has got to be stopped,' said Sir Edward curtly. 'These people are dangerous — the more dangerous because they are obviously international. They are working for no particular country. They have got to be found — the heads, the people in control.' He passed his hand wearily across his forehead. 'We must go carefully. There have been leakages. They have agents everywhere. The people in control may be high up — people you'd never suspect. That is why the plan we agreed upon seemed to offer the best chance of success . . . ' He broke off and crushed his half-smoked cigarette in the ashtray. 'If only Magda Vettrilli had had time to speak . . . '

The Chief of Staff said nothing but continued to mechanically polish the blackened bowl of his pipe.

'That's all,' said Sir Edward curtly.

The Chief of Staff got up quietly and left the office. The blonde secretary looked up as he passed to his own room. Usually he smiled at her. Today, he went by without taking any notice of her at all.

She shrugged her shoulders.

V

Kettleby sat at a round iron table in front of a café with a yellow awning in the Little Socco. Before him was a vile mixture that was supposed to be coffee — a muddy brew that tasted horrible. Noise surrounded him, a hideous din compounded of a babble of voices, the bells of donkeys, the cries of merchants, and the toot of motor horns. Smells, difficult to analyse, wafted about him on the slight breeze, and dust blew from the top of the iron table.

It was ten o'clock in the morning and Kettleby had been sitting at that table since half past nine. His stained linen suit was more crumpled than ever, his panama limper and more battered. He looked dejected and rather ill. His hand, when he lifted the coffee, was shaking slightly. The throng that passed in the narrow street glanced at him contemptuously. He fumbled in the pocket of his jacket and brought out a carton of cheap cigarettes. He lit one and threw away the match, letting the cigarette dangle limply from his lips.

He was sitting here at the table in front of the café with the yellow awning because he had been instructed to sit here every morning from ten until a quarter past in case Scott should want to see Marchment, but his mind was busy with a problem that had suddenly cropped up.

He wasn't quite sure how to act. It was quite by chance that he had stumbled on what he believed was a clue to the identity of the 'Faceless Ones.' And yet it was so absolutely incredible that he couldn't make up his mind what he ought to do.

Should he report his discovery, or should he make absolutely sure before laying himself open to ridicule?

If he could find out on his own — obtain irrefutable proof — before disclosing his discoveries to anyone it would be a feather in his cap.

Long dormant ambitions began to stir within him. Enthusiasms that he had had to suppress, tugged softly, but with increasing urgency, at his heart-strings.

If he could pull this off by himself . . .

He felt a slight increase in the rate of his pulse beats. The prospect was an alluring one. Perhaps, if he pulled this off, the Department would be sufficiently grateful to grant him a transfer. For four years he had endured the noise and the smells of Tangier, living in a stuffy little room at the top of a cheap hotel, and building up a reputation for being a poverty-stricken drunk. He hated it all, the shabby stained suit, the whole character of the man he was portraying.

He drank some of the vile decoction called coffee that was now lukewarm, and fumbled in his jacket pocket for his cigarettes. Lighting one with a shaking hand, the shake had become almost second nature by now, he inhaled and let the smoke dribble out through his nostrils.

He would have to be very careful. If he made a false move he knew the fate that awaited him — the same fate that had overtaken Magda.

He sat on at the little table, oblivious of the noise and the smells and the heat, considering his plans . . .

VI

At the top of a large square tower near the edge of the Kasbah, drinking mint tea, Egerton Scott sat at a round table and looked out over the parapet at the Mediterranean.

In Tangier's land-locked harbour several ships were anchored, cargo ships, a passenger ship, and a long-hulled graceful yacht, further out in the bay.

It was one of the largest private motor yachts that Scott had ever seen, and he concluded, from the name on her bows, that it belonged to the American millionairess, Alison Mae Swanson, who had thrown the party at the Cosmo Club on the previous night. The M.Y. *Cygnet*. Scott smiled in appreciation.

There was nobody but himself on the tower, and an elderly Arab in a white *jalebah* who drowsed under his peaked hood under the stairs some way off. It was quiet, and Scott wanted quiet. His cogitations of the night before had produced no tangible result. He was still uncertain what move to make.

A thundering brick wall, that's what he found he was up against. Something had *got* to be done. And the only thing that seemed likely to lead to any results was the rather risky plan of deliberately drawing attention to himself. If he started asking questions about Magda, these unknown people would get suspicious. They would do something. They wouldn't be able to ignore this stranger who was beginning to probe and peer into things and they would take some kind of steps in the matter. They might, thought Scott wrily, not be very pleasant steps, but that was part of his job. Any steps at all were better than nothing. He would offer himself as the bait, and hope that he could avoid being hooked.

He finished his mint tea and went down the steps of the tower. He had, earlier that morning, bought a small car, as Marchment had suggested, and he drove back slowly along the teeming streets of Tangier.

As he pulled up at a tobacco shop and got out of the car, he caught sight of the shabby figure of Kettleby shambling along on the other side of the street. The panama was pulled down over his eyes and he appeared to be oblivious of his surroundings. What a game this was, thought Scott. How the fellow must hate the role he had to play day after day, week after week. People imagined that working for the British Security Service was like it was depicted in sensational fiction. Luxurious living and the company of beautiful and seductive women! Whereas, it was mostly drab and boring, with the prospect of a knife or a bullet in your back at the end of it. There was precious little glamour and less kudos!

He bought a box of fifty Piccadilly cigarettes and was leaving the shop when a thought struck him.

'Give me a box of ordinary safety matches and a box with the red tips that will strike on anything,' he said.

The Arab shopkeeper supplied his needs with grave politeness, and Scott went back to his car. A hail greeted him as he twisted the handle of the driving seat door.

'Lo' bud,' cried a voice. 'How did yer make out at the Flamenco, hey? If you got away still wearin' yer socks, you're a lucky guy.'

It was the American sailor who had directed him.

'Bit of a low dive, isn't it?' said Scott.

'There're worse, but not much,' declared the sailor. 'Still, I'll say Tangier's got what it takes. Suits me okay.'

'Been here long?' asked Scott.

The sailor removed the wrapping from a strip of chewing gum.

'Best part of a month,' he said. 'I reckon they can make it another month, buddy. I guess, this is the kinda job I can take a lot of.'

'Which ship are you from?' inquired Scott.

'M.Y. *Cygnet*,' answered the sailor, slipping the unwrapped gum into his mouth and thrusting it into one cheek. 'A dandy little craft — and a dandy little owner, too.'

He grinned and winked.

'Mrs. Alison Swanson, you mean?' said Scott. 'I saw her at a party at the Cosmo . . . '

The sailor made a gesture.

'Party,' he grunted disgustedly. 'I brought 'em ashore in the launch. What a gang of kill-joys! One foot in the morgue, an' the other on the edge, eh? What a goodlookin' dame like Alison wants to tote about with those guys an' dolls for, sure beats me.'

'Mostly millionaires, I hear,' said Scott.

'That shouldn't worry little Alison,' retorted the sailor. 'She's got all the dollars in the world! Why doesn't she get up a *real* party — guys with a bit of life? You'd sure think they was at Pat Malony's wake!'

'I suppose you get plenty of time off?' said Scott.

'I told yer, bud, it's a good job,' grinned the sailor. 'I gotta call on a little floosey I picked up last night. Nifty bit o' stuff! Be seein' yer.'

He waved a hand like a small ham and walked quickly away.

Egerton Scott was at a loose end. He didn't want to go back to the hotel for lunch. Marchment had mentioned the Hassan Tower on the outskirts of Rabat. He decided that he'd drive over to Rabat and inspect the place. He had no idea of the way and it might be necessary at some future time to get there quickly. He had bought a fairly good map of the district at the same time that he'd bought the car, and this he studied.

Calling at a café, he bought some sandwiches and a bottle of wine, and, supplied with all the necessaries for a picnic lunch, set out on his journey.

Death lurked in the old ruin of the Hassan Tower, but he had no pre-knowledge of this as he took the coast road and drove steadily out of Tangier.

4

I

Scott enjoyed the drive along the coast. The day was hot and sunny, the sky a dome of hazy blue that was reflected in the sea. Half-way on his journey he stopped to eat some of the sandwiches he had brought with him and drink the light white wine. It would have been better colder, but he was glad of it, even in its tepid condition, for the heat had made him thirsty. He ate his lunch in the grateful shade of a patch of trees, and was reluctant to leave the comparative coolness.

It was fairly late in the afternoon before he reached his destination. The distance from Tangier was quite appreciable.

The Hassan Tower was an ancient ruin, isolated and deserted. Piles of weed-covered stones, that had fallen from the original edifice, littered the immediate vicinity, and against one of these, Scott settled himself with his rolled-up jacket for a back rest.

It would be nice, he thought, as he lit a cigarette and relaxed, if he were really here on holiday. If there was no job of work niggling at the back of his mind. The world was a very pleasant place. Everything for the pleasure and delight of man had been put at his disposal — if he had the sense to enjoy it. But he hadn't. *Those whom the gods would destroy they first make mad.* Who had said that? Scott couldn't remember, but it seemed to him that it was only too true. Surely only mad people would devote their brains and enormous sums of money to bring about their own destruction? And the destruction of the whole of civilization . . .

Civilization?

Was there such a thing? Central heating, better drainage, chromium plate — that didn't make for civilization. Civilization was an attitude of mind, a standard of living that had little to do with material advantages.

When you came to think of it — *really*

think of it — what a lot of insane nonsense the whole thing was. Everybody in fear of somebody else. Suspicion, hatred, desire for power. Bigger and better bombs, greater and more sweeping ways of wiping out mankind, quicker and easier methods of scattering the earth to dust.

The pressure on a button, an accident, a mistake, and the terror would be unleashed. And the fate of mankind lay in the hands of a comparative few. There would be only a limited number of survivals once the chain of death and destruction had been started. Those who, in readiness for the debacle, had scuttled to the deep hideouts they had prepared. The ordinary normal members of the community, the reasonable people who worked and played, loved and had children, went to the local for a pint of beer, did all the small, everyday things that were the joy of living, they would be blasted out of existence or left to die a lingering death from the aftermath.

This was the prospect that all the cleverness of this scientific age offered as a heritage . . .

Egerton Scott threw away the stub of his cigarette and reached out his hand for the bottle of wine which he had brought from the car. It was still half-full and he drew the cork.

He heard the 'ping' of the bullet as it struck the bottle and the vicious whine as it ricochetted past his head. The sound of the report followed almost instantly. A second shot brought splinters of stone from the pile against which he was sitting.

Scott dropped the shattered bottle and wriggled round in the shelter of the stones.

Somebody was shooting at him from the base of the tower! He peered cautiously round the heap of stones, and a third shot struck the ground near his face, spurting up soil into his eyes. He rubbed it away and saw a thin wisp of smoke curling sluggishly into the still air.

He felt in the holster under his shirt and drew out his own small automatic. He thumbed down the safety-catch and rolled over on to his stomach.

There were no more shots, but he couldn't be sure that it was safe to venture from his cover. The unknown shooter was probably waiting for just that.

Scott allowed several minutes to pass and then, when there was no further sign of the unknown, he began to edge his way through the weeds, that grew thickly, towards a second pile of stones. He expected every second to hear the whine of a bullet past his face but nothing of the sort happened. He reached the shelter of the stone heap and cautiously raised his head. Everything at the tower was quite silent. There was no vestige of sound or movement.

Gripping his automatic, Scott rose to a crouching position. And suddenly there came to his ears the staccato roar of a motor bicycle engine.

It revved up, and a big machine shot out of the shadow on the other side of the tower and went racing away along the road.

Scott only had a vague impression of the figure crouching over the handlebars before machine and rider disappeared in a cloud of dust.

He straightened up and brushed himself down. The incident had been quite unexpected, and he was puzzled to account for it. These people couldn't suspect him, surely? And yet there was no other explanation for the shots. They had been intended for him without a doubt. But how did the shooter *know* that he was coming to the Hassan Tower that day? He had made up his mind on the spur of the moment and he had told no one. He must have been followed, but he had seen nobody.

He took out a cigarette and lit it, drawing in the smoke gratefully. The whole thing had been rather a shock, and it gave rise to a distinctly unpleasant thought. If these people knew what he was, they must have been tipped off. And that meant somebody in the Department.

A very unpleasant thought indeed.

Frowning, Scott walked over to the tower. He had intended exploring it after his rest, and he decided to do so without further delay.

He moved slowly round the base until he came to the place where the motor cycle had come from. Near this spot he caught sight of something on the ground that glistened in the sun. Stooping, he picked it up. It was the spent shell of a .32 calibre automatic. A few yards away was another. It was from here that the unknown had fired.

Egerton Scott searched the place thoroughly, but beyond two more shells there was nothing. He moved over to the broken entrance to the old tower — a crumbling archway that had probably once been fitted with a door. Beyond the arch was deep shadow, but the sunlight fell half-across the threshold in a sharp slant.

And just touched by the edge of the light was a foot!

Scott drew in his breath quickly. The foot was clad in an expensive shoe — a man's shoe . . .

He stepped quickly into the shadow of the arch. It was not so dark within as it had looked from outside. The reflection of the sunlight shed a dim glow — sufficient for him to see the man who sprawled on his back in a pool of blood that was almost dry.

It was John P. Ogden and he was dead!

II

The American had been shot twice at close range. The white silk shirt front was burnt and blackened round the places where the bullets had entered. There was little blood on the front. The blood had come from the exit wounds in the back.

Egerton Scott made sure that the man was quite dead before he straightened up and decided what he ought to do. His first inclination was to drive into Rabat and inform the police of his discovery, but on second thoughts he discarded the idea. It might lead to a lot of unpleasant complications. He might well be suspected of shooting the American himself. It was known that they had been acquainted in Tangier. They had been seen together at the Cosmo Club, and they were both staying at the same hotel.

No, it would be better to keep clear. He could telephone the police at Rabat and notify them that there was a dead body in the old Hassan Tower and let them get on with it. A more important consideration, from his point of view, was the reason why Ogden had been murdered.

Who and what had Ogden been? Was he part of the unknown group or was he working on the other side? An American counterpart of Scott, perhaps?

He knelt down again by the inert body and carefully went through the pockets of the light suit. There was a bulky wallet stuffed with various kinds of currency, a bunch of keys, a gold ball-pointed pen and pencil, a passport in the name of John P. Ogden with a photograph of the dead man and a Connecticut address, and that was all. If there had been anything else it had been taken by the murderer.

And then Scott saw the matchbox!

It lay against the stone wall, just out of the line of sunlight. He could quite easily have missed it. Stooping, he picked it up. It was an ordinary matchbox, but within it was not so ordinary. It contained two safey matches and three with red heads!

The counterpart of the matchbox which Magda Vettrilli had been clutching in her hand when she had been shot dead on the steps of the British Consulate.

How had it got there? Had it come from Ogden's pocket or had it been dropped by the murderer?

Egerton Scott put it carefully in his pocket. If there had been any doubt before that the murder of the American was linked with the shooting of Magda, and the business which had brought him, Scott, to Tangier, the discovery of the matchbox settled it.

The question was, what did the matchbox mean? This wasn't so difficult to answer as it had been. The obvious answer was that it was some kind of passport or identity label. A member of the unknown group could make himself known to another member by the production of the matchbox. Was this the true meaning of the matchbox? Scott was pretty certain that it was. Some such idea had been hovering at the back of his mind for some time.

Was that all the significance attached to the matchbox? Or was there something deeper? It was difficult to form any conclusion at the moment, and, he thought, the quicker he got away from the

Hassan Tower the better. Somebody might come along the road and see him there . . .

He gave a quick glance round and came out into the sunlight which seemed twice as bright after the gloom. As he came round the base of the tower he heard the sound of an approaching car, and stopped. Better to let it go past before he went in search of his own.

But it did not go past! It slowed down and pulled up!

Scott muttered a curse under his breath. Sightseers, he supposed. They might be here for a long time. He'd better risk it, get in his car, and start back for Tangier.

Slowly he walked out of the cover of the tower toward the place where he had left his car. The other car had stopped close by it, and a girl was getting out.

Egerton Scott noted that she was a very pretty, dark-haired girl and that, apparently, there was nobody else in the small car because she shut the door firmly before she turned away.

She saw Scott and, to his surprise,

came over to meet him.

'I'm Jeanette Dupris,' she announced with the trace of an accent. 'You are Mr. John P. Ogden, aren't you?'

III

Egerton Scott thought quickly. This attractive girl, who was obviously French, had come here to meet the American. Quite certainly she had never met Ogden before or she would not have mistaken *him* for Ogden. If he allowed the mistake to continue, he might learn something important.

'Good afternoon, Miss Dupris,' he said. 'I'm glad you came . . . '

'It would have been easier for me to meet you in Tangier,' she replied. Except for that very faint and rather attractive accent her English was perfect. 'But you insisted that it would be safer.'

But poor Ogden had been wrong, thought Scott. It *hadn't* been safer . . . Aloud, he said:

'I guess, that's right.'

He waited for her to continue.

'There's not very much I can tell you,' she went on after a slight pause. 'Magda and I were friends, you understand, but she didn't talk about herself much.'

'I see,' said Scott. He had got the clue he sought. This girl had been a friend of Magda Vettrilli's, Ogden had discovered this and had arranged to meet her with the object of gathering information. So far so good. 'I suppose her death was a shock to you?'

'Indeed it was,' declared the girl. 'It was terrible. I would do anything to help find the people who killed her. Magda was very kind to me when I was in trouble . . . '

She broke off and her eyes filled with tears. He wondered just what Ogden had already said to her. How had he explained his interest in Magda Vettrilli's murder? She answered his unspoken question almost as though he had put it into words.

'You're acting for her relations, aren't you?' she said. 'It was a surprise to me that she had a mother in America. She never mentioned it.'

So *that's* what Ogden had told her?

'I believe there was some kind of estrangement,' he said evasively. 'How long had you known Miss Vettrilli?'

'Over a year,' she answered. 'I was working at the Cosmo Club then — in charge of the cloak room.'

Egerton Scott's eyes strayed to the expensive little car that had brought her from Tangier. She saw the look and smiled.

'You're wondering how I can afford the car?' she said. 'I couldn't. I borrowed it from a friend. What kind of questions do you want to ask me about Magda? I don't know very much. I told you that on the telephone.'

'I should like to know *anything* you can tell me about Miss Vettrilli — particularly anything about the day that she met her death.'

'I never saw her that day,' she replied. 'I saw her the day previously — in the evening at the Orange Orchid — and she seemed a little, how shall I put it? distrait. Several times while I was talking to her she asked me to repeat what I had said. You know, as though she were thinking of something else.'

'She didn't explain why?'

Jeanette Dupris shook her head.

'No,' she answered. 'I asked her what was the matter. I thought she was worried about something . . . '

'Where,' asked Scott, 'is the Orange Orchid?'

'It's a little café in the rue Waller,' she said. 'Magda and I often used to go there for a meal.'

'And she didn't tell you why she was — worried?'

'I am not sure that she *was* worried,' replied the girl. 'It was only the impression I got from her behaviour. But I'm quite sure she wasn't herself. She was facing something that made her uneasy. We were going to the cinema after our dinner, but she said she had a headache and went home.'

'Had she many friends?' asked Scott.

'I don't quite know how to answer that,' said the girl thoughtfully. 'She knew quite a lot of people but I wouldn't say that she had many real friends.'

'You're French, aren't you?' he asked suddenly.

She looked surprised. 'Yes. Why do you ask?'

'You speak such good English,' he said, and she laughed.

'I was educated in England,' she said. 'I spent most of my childhood there. Both my parents were killed in an accident and I came out to Tangier to my uncle. He died three years ago.'

'And you remained in Tangier ever since?'

'Yes. I like Tangier,' she said. 'But you didn't ask me to come all this way to talk about me, did you?'

'I guess not,' admitted Scott. 'Did your friend, Magda, have any special boy friend?'

'No, there was nothing serious in that way. She liked Enrico Silvo quite a bit, I think.'

'The leader of the Guitarist Band at the Cosmo Club?'

She nodded.

'But if you imagine that there was any real love affair in her life,' she added quickly, 'I mean, that would account for the — the murder, I'm sure you're mistaken.'

'I wasn't thinking that,' said Scott truthfully.

She looked at him steadily. He thought that she had very beautiful eyes.

'What exactly are you, Mr. Ogden?' she asked. 'Are you connected with the police — the American police, I mean?'

He shook his head.

'No,' he answered. 'I'm nothing to do with the police.'

'But there's something more in it than just inquiring about Magda on behalf of her mother, isn't there? I'm not a fool, you know. Unless there was something more behind it, why all this secrecy? Why bring me out here to see you? You said it was safer. Safer from what?'

Egerton Scott took several seconds before he replied. Then he took the plunge.

'Miss Dupris,' he said seriously, 'you must prepare yourself for a shock. I am not John P. Ogden, the man you were expecting to meet . . . '

Her eyes hardened.

'What do you mean?' she demanded.

'John P. Ogden is dead,' said Scott rapidly. 'Listen, and I'll explain . . . '

Briefly, he told her the truth and her expression changed from anger to incredulity as she listened.

'How do I know that what you say is true?' she demanded when he had finished. 'Why should I believe you? You lied about being Mr. Ogden, why shouldn't you be lying now?'

'No reason at all,' said Scott candidly. 'Except that I'm not! What I've told you is absolutely true.'

Her eyes searched his face. There was shrewdness behind their clear depth. Her first remark showed that she was practical.

'I'll believe you,' she said suddenly. 'Now, we'd better go, hadn't we? Anybody may come here at any moment and find — *him* . . . '

'I agree,' answered Scott. 'Can I see you in Tangier — later tonight?'

'Where?'

'How about the Orange Orchid?' he suggested. 'We could have dinner together . . . ?'

'All right.' She nodded quickly. 'I'll be there at a quarter to nine.

'I'll be waiting for you,' he promised. 'Just in case anything should stop you coming, where can I find you?'

She opened her handbag, took out a letter, removed the envelope, and gave it to him.

'That's my address,' she said, and added with a smile: 'You can see that my name is really Jeanette Dupris!'

Before he could reply, she ran lightly across to her car, slipped into the driving seat, and was gone.

Egerton Scott went over to his own car. He had taken a chance in telling this girl the truth. He knew very well that if he had made a mistake in his judgment of her it might easily cost him his life.

5

I

Egerton Scott stopped on the way back to
Tangier and telephoned to the Commandant of Police at Rabat. Briefly, he stated
that there was a dead man in the old
Hassan Tower, and rang off before
the excited Belgian at the other end of the
wire could ask any questions. It was up to
the police to do their own investigations,
and he had no wish to get mixed up in
the matter if he could avoid it.

John P. Ogden had come to Tangier on
the same errand as himself. That was
pretty obvious. And he had discovered
something that had sealed his death
warrant. Was it the girl, Jeanette Dupris?
Had the Group discovered that he was in
communication with her and were they
afraid that she might pass on to him
important information concerning them?

If that were the case, she must know

92

something, but she didn't appear to. She had been a friend of Magda's, but Magda had told her nothing. Or had she? Perhaps Jeanette knew something that she wasn't *aware* that she knew — something that was important to the safety of 'Group X' but which didn't appear to be important. Or again Jeanette might be one of them.

If she were, he, Scott, had really stuck his neck out and the result would be swift and certain.

These people had no compunction in taking any steps to ensure their own safety. He would have to be very watchful if he wanted to survive.

And yet he couldn't bring himself to believe that Jeanette was not on the level. Because she was an unusually attractive girl? No, it wasn't that. He had dealt with women equally as attractive. It was that there was something about her that was innately honest and open. She was genuinely anxious to do all she could to help in finding the people who had killed her friend, and, if they were aware of this, she was in considerable danger herself.

So Magda had been particularly friendly with Enrico Silvo, the band leader, had she? Maybe that was a line worth following up. It was possible that he might be mixed up in the affair. If Magda had suspected that he knew anything about the group she would naturally have cultivated his friendship.

When he entered the vestibule of the Minzeh Hotel there was a difference in the usual atmosphere, an air of suppressed excitement, that told him that the news of Ogden's murder had already reached there. Two Arab policemen stood near the reception desk, and the manager was talking to the clerk.

Scott, ignoring them, went across to the lift. He noticed that they all turned to stare at him before he was whisked up to his own floor. It had been known that he had been friendly with the American, and naturally they would want to question him.

In this he was right, because he hadn't been in his room more than a few minutes before there was a knock at the door and the manager, accompanied by an Inspector of Police and a Commandant, entered.

The manager was full of apologies. He was sorry that Mr. Scott should be disturbed, but a terrible thing had happened. The American gentleman, Mr. Ogden, had been killed. He had been shot, and it was obviously a case of murder. The police would like to ask Mr. Scott a few questions. It was very inconvenient and unfortunate, but necessary. He hoped that Mr. Scott would understand. It was a dreadful thing to have happened to a guest at the hotel. Such a thing had never happened before, etc.

Mr. Scott assured the manager that he quite understood. It was indeed a terrible thing. How had it happened — here in the hotel?

The Commandant of Police took over before the excited manager could reply. He expressed his profound regret at having to disturb Mr. Scott over this unfortunate affair but he understood that Mr. Scott had been a friend of the dead man . . . ?

'You understand wrongly,' said Egerton, shaking his head. 'Mr. Ogden was merely a passenger on the plane from Lisbon with me. We had both booked at this hotel. That is all.'

The Commandant, who spoke almost faultless English, seemed disappointed.

'You spent the evening together,' he said.

'Yesterday evening,' said Scott. 'Yes. I wanted to go to the Cosmo Club. I discovered that it was a membership club only. Mr. Ogden was a member and very kindly asked me to dine there as his guest.'

'You know nothing about his private affairs?' asked the Commandant. 'You cannot suggest any reason why he should have been shot, or who would have wanted to kill him?'

'I can't tell you anything about him at all,' declared Scott. 'I understood that he was a business man who very often came to Tangier in connection with his business. I don't even know what that business was.'

'Had he other friends?'

'I *wasn't* a friend,' said Egerton firmly. 'I was, as I've told you, only an acquaintance. He may have had many friends, but I can't tell you who they were. I didn't see him with anyone during the very short time I knew him.'

The Commandant was thoughtful. He said, after a slight pause:

'You have been out all day, Mr. Scott?'

'Yes, I was out in my car,' replied Egerton.

'Where did you go?' asked the Commandant quickly.

'I was just driving about Tangier,' answered Scott. 'Up the old Mountain Road and generally round the outskirts.'

'You didn't go near the old Hassan Tower at Rabat?' The Commandant shot the question sharply.

'No. What is that?' said Scott with a slightly puzzled expression. 'Is it something special?'

'It is an old ruin,' said the Commandant. 'It is where this man, Ogden, was found dead . . . '

'Are you suggesting,' demanded Scott angrily, 'that I had anything to do with his death?'

'No, no, please do not misunderstand,' said the Commandant, spreading his hands apologetically. 'I am only trying to discover the truth. This American was shot at the Tower, and someone, a man, rang up the police at Rabat and told them that this had happened . . . '

'Somebody rang the police at Rabat, did they?' said Scott. 'Who?'

The Commandant shrugged his shoulders.

'That we do not know,' he said. 'We would like to know. The police at Rabat found the body with the dead man's passport. They communicated with us, here in Tangier . . . '

'I wish I could help you,' said Scott, 'but you know as much about the unfortunate man as I do.'

'I am full of unhappiness that you should have been troubled,' declared the manager. 'The police are not good for my hotel. It is most unfortunate that this American should have been staying here.'

'We shall not disturb you longer,' said the Commandant graciously. 'I offer you a thousand apologies but, you understand, I have my duty to do . . . '

He bowed, the manager bowed, the Inspector bowed. Finally they bowed themselves out of the room and Egerton Scott gave a sigh of relief.

He poured himself out a generous helping of John Haig and drank it neat. He felt that he needed something to steady his nerves. The police were the least of his worries, though it could be decidedly awkward if they discovered that he *had* been in the vicinity of the Hassan Tower that afternoon.

He went into the bathroom, took a shower, and changed his clothes. He wondered what his dinner with Jeanette would bring forth, if anything. Sitting down in an easy chair, he examined the matchbox that he had found near Ogden's body. But there was nothing more to be discovered about it. He put it carefully in his pocket, lighted a cigarette, and poured himself out another John Haig . . .

II

It was half past eight when he entered the little café in the rue Waller where he had arranged to meet Jeanette Dupris. It was quite a small place, but clean and pleasantly decorated. There were not many customers and he had no difficulty in finding a table that was fairly secluded in one corner. It had the advantage of allowing him to see the whole restaurant with a solid wall behind him. Experience had taught him the value of that.

'I'll order presently,' he said to the waiter who came over to him. 'I'm expecting a lady. You can bring me a pink gin while I'm waiting — Plymouth gin and only a dash of Angostura.'

The waiter deposited the menu on the table and went away. Egerton Scott surveyed the other customers with apparent indifference. They were a mixed lot, all foreigners, and seemed to be intent on the food before them. There was a curtained archway on the left of the oblong room through which the waiter had disappeared, and Scott concluded that it led to the kitchen department.

In a remarkably short time the waiter returned with the pink gin. Scott poured in a little iced water and tasted it. It was excellent — just the right mixture. It was surprising how few places could mix a really good pink gin. Either there was too much Angostura or the wrong gin.

He leaned back in his chair and lighted a cigarette. It would be a quarter of an hour before Jeanette arrived — even if she were punctual.

He was just stubbing out his cigarette when the door opened and the woman who called herself Lady Boynton-Smith came in. She paused inside the entrance and gazed arrogantly round the restaurant. She was dressed in a black cocktail dress that enhanced the bony structure of her body and the sallowness of her horse-like face. She selected a vacant table, sat down, and deposited her handbag and gloves on the other chair. Superciliously she inspected the rest of the customers, eyeing them as though they were specimens of strange and unusual insects. Finally, her gold-rimmed glasses came to rest on Egerton Scott. She gave him only a brief glance and then, as the waiter appeared through the archway, she called to him in her high, imperious, strident voice.

'I want some melon followed by veal cutlets, new potatoes, and French beans,' she said waving away the menu. 'And I expect them all to be properly cooked! If they are not, I shall refuse to pay for them, you understand?'

The waiter spread his hands and murmured something that Scott didn't catch.

'No, no, perfectly plain,' said Lady Boynton-Smith. 'I dislike sauces of all kinds. They disguise the freshness of the meat. You may bring me a Martini, and see that it is very dry.'

She dismissed the waiter, picked up her bag and extracted a thin, gold cigarette case. From this she took a cigarette, lit it with a lighter, and blew out a stream of smoke.

Scott watched her with interest. Who was this woman who had pretended to be Lady Boynton-Smith at the Cosmo? Was she just an ordinary tourist who imagined that a title would impress people, or was there something more behind the imposture?

He was still wondering when Jeanette came in. He rose as she came over to his table, and he pulled out her chair. She sat down with a smile.

'I'm sorry to be late,' she said, 'but I had to finish some work.'

'Fifteen minutes for a woman can hardly be called late,' answered Scott. 'What would you like as an aperitif?'

'Sherry, please,' she said. 'Medium dry.'

Scott beckoned to the waiter. He saw that the eyes of Lady Boynton-Smith were fixed inquisitively on him — a hard stare that some people might have found disconcerting.

'Bring me a medium dry sherry — Findlater's Dry Fly, if you have it — and another Plymouth pink gin,' he ordered and as the waiter went away: 'What was the work you had to finish?'

'I design hats,' she said. 'And make them, too. I haven't a shop, I do the work in my flat. Most of my customers are regulars, you see.'

'That kind of work requires nourishment,' said Scott. He picked up the menu. 'Are you hungry?'

'Yes, I am,' she said frankly. 'The entrecote steaks are very good here . . . '

'Then we'll try them,' said Scott. 'With sauté potatoes and fresh peas — how's that?'

She nodded.

'I see,' he went on, 'that they've got some of those very succulent Portuguese prawns. Do you like them?'

'Very much,' she said.

'Then we'll start with those, and for a sweet we might have fresh pineapple with Kirsch . . . '

'Delicious!' agreed Jeanette.

'That's settled,' said Scott.

The waiter came back with their drinks, and Egerton gave the order. Jeanette said she would rather have some Vichy water, instead of wine, so Scott ordered half a bottle of claret for himself.

'The service is a little slow here,' said Jeanette, 'but the cooking is excellent.'

'I'm not in any hurry unless you are?' he said.

She laughed.

'My time is yours — until midnight,' she replied.

'Cinderella, eh?' he said.

She laughed again, but she didn't explain why she was only free until midnight.

'Did you — did you tell the police?' she asked in a low voice. He nodded.

'Yes. They've been to my hotel. I think they were satisfied that Ogden was only an acquaintance. I hope they were, anyhow!'

'It's all dreadful.' She frowned and her fingers moved restlessly round the stem of her sherry glass. 'Poor Magda and now Mr. Ogden . . . '

'And possibly me, if I'm not careful,' said Scott. 'These people are quite ruthless. Which reminds me, you'd better be extra careful yourself.'

She looked at him quickly.

'Me?' she said.

He nodded.

'They must know that Ogden made that appointment with you at the Hassan Tower,' he explained. 'If they think you know anything — that Magda may have dropped some hint that would be dangerous to them . . . '

'I see what you mean,' she broke in. 'You know, you make me feel scared . . . '

'It would be foolish to pretend that there's no danger,' he answered. 'In all probability we are both being watched . . . '

'I don't think I feel *quite* so hungry now,' said Jeanette. She drank some of her sherry. 'Haven't you any idea who these people are?'

He shook his head.

'Not the faintest,' he declared candidly. 'But I believe that Magda knew. Didn't she say *anything* that might give me a pointer?'

'I've been trying to think,' said the girl, knitting her brows, 'but I can't remember anything at all. Except — no, that couldn't be anything . . . '

'Tell me,' he said quickly.

'It was several weeks ago,' answered Jeanette. 'I called in to see her at her flat one evening. She'd asked me to bring her a new hat. She was writing down a list of names on a pad . . . '

'A list of names?' interrupted Scott. 'But this may be the very thing I'm after . . . '

'I don't see how it could be,' she said. 'They were girls Christian names. You know, Sally, Vera, Janice, Mary, Kate, Alice — there was a whole column of them. I asked her what she was doing and she said that she was looking for a name for a child . . . '

Scott looked his disappointment.

'A name for a child?' he repeated. 'Why was she doing that?'

'One of her friends had just had a baby and she was going to suggest some names,' replied Jeanette. 'I told you there was really nothing helpful.'

Scott was forced to agree. There was nothing helpful there — unless . . . ?

'Who was the friend?' he asked suddenly.

'She didn't say,' answered Jeanette.

'You didn't know of any friend of hers who had just had a child?'

She shook her head.

'So that it could have been an excuse,' he went on. 'To account for the list of names?'

'I suppose it could,' she agreed doubtfully. 'But what could a list of girls names mean?'

'I don't know.' He sighed ruefully. 'Only it's something *odd*, isn't it?'

Jeanette finished the remainder of her

sherry. She opened her mouth to say something when the waiter arrived to serve their dinner and she stopped.

It was an excellent meal, well cooked, the steaks tender and grilled to a turn. Scott would have enjoyed it more if his mind had not been busy trying to find an explanation for what the girl had told him. The high, strident voice of the pseudo Lady Boynton-Smith, complaining that her veal cutlets had been over-cooked, distracted his attention. That was something else that required an explanation. Who was the woman? Did she fit in somehow, or was her masquerade pure snobbery? He would have to look further into the matter of 'Lady Boynton-Smith.' As though she had read his thoughts, she shot him a malignant look, before returning to her attack on the unfortunate waiter.

Jeanette was looking at him with a slight smile.

'You *are* a long way away,' she said a little reproachfully. 'If you worry while you eat your food you will get indigestion before you are middle-aged.'

'I'm sorry,' he apologized and, with an

effort, he put all thought of the reason why he was dining with this very attractive girl out of his mind and concentrated on being an attentive and amusing host. He succeeded so well that it was after eleven before they both realized how late it had got.

When he had taken the girl home — she lived in a small flat over a shop that sold souvenirs for tourists in the rue Cintra — and arranged that she should meet him on the following evening, he went back to the hotel, deciding that there were other and more exciting interests in life than running to earth an unknown and illusive organization known as 'Group X.'

That it loomed very largely in his immediate future he discovered when he unlocked the door of his room and switched on the light.

III

The room, which should have been empty, was not!

Sitting in the armchair, turned round

so that it faced the door, was a man. He was not a very pleasant looking man. His face was lean and of a dead whiteness that was enhanced by the jet blackness of his hair.

His eyes held no expression at all. They were of a pale blue that made him look curiously blind. In a thin hand, the fingers of which were stained with tobacco, he held a small automatic pistol. His wrist rested on his crossed knees. He looked at Scott without the slightest trace of interest.

'What the devil are you doing in my room?' demanded Scott, recovering from his first surprise at this unexpected reception committee of one.

'I want to talk to you,' replied the visitor in a low voice that had a queer hissing quality, as unpleasant as the rest of him.

'If you don't get out at once,' snapped Scott. 'I shall ring and have you put out . . . '

'I don't think so,' said the other. 'You will be dead before your finger leaves the bell-button.'

There was no intonation at all in that hissing voice, but the effect was deadly. Egerton Scott knew that the man meant every word.

'And what do you suppose would happen to *you*?' he asked.

'That is a matter of complete indifference to me,' was the answer. And he meant that, too. There was a moment's silence. Into this unreal silence the hissing voice dripped like ice:

'I suggest that you sit down and listen.'

'What is this exactly?' said Egerton, sitting on the side of the bed. 'A new kind of hold-up?'

'Merely a word of warning,' replied the other. 'If you are a wise man you will heed it. It will not be repeated.'

'I don't know what you mean,' said Scott. 'You must have come to the wrong room. I'm in Tangier on holiday . . . '

'Why lie? We know why you are here. We know what you have come here to do . . . '

'Who's *we*?' demanded Scott. 'Surely there aren't any more of you?'

'We are legion,' answered the white-faced

man. 'Our numbers grow every day, every hour. Go back to England.'

'And if I refuse?'

With a swift, reptilian movement the man was on his feet. Without changing the level tone of his voice, he said:

'There is a plane leaving for Lisbon in the morning. If you are not on it you're a dead man! I am not threatening — I am stating a fact!'

'Nasty things facts,' said Scott coolly. 'I always hated 'em when I was at school! And they're not always right. What was thought to be a fact a few years ago, isn't a fact any longer . . . '

'I have said what I came to say,' said the other. 'What you do is your own affair. But if you are still in Tangier by midday tomorrow you will stay for ever.'

He walked coolly over to the door and opened it.

'Don't try to follow me,' he warned. 'I am being covered, and it would be dangerous for you.'

The next second, he had slipped out of the door and shut it behind him.

Scott made a movement to follow and

thought better of it. What good would it do? The man's retreat was certainly well-planned — like his arrival. These people would see to that.

He went over to the tray of whisky and glasses, poured out a very stiff John Haig and drank it.

The finding of the white-faced man sitting in his chair when he put on the light had been a shock. He had expected a more drastic ending. He lit a cigarette and sat down.

Why had they troubled to warn him?

They must have some very good reason for that. It would have been quite simple to shoot him there and then. Why hadn't they done that? He could find no satisfactory answer.

'We are legion.' That's what the white-faced man had said. A vast and widespread organization that covered every country in the world, controlled by a central control — the head of the Hydra. And that central control, according to the Department, had its headquarters in Tangier.

And there was somebody in this central control who was very well informed indeed! Somebody who knew who and what he was and why he was in Tangier. And that meant a leak — in fact a great, hefty gash in the Department itself. The leader, or leaders, of 'Group X' were being tipped off. Possibly that was how they had discovered Magda . . .

He must get hold of Marchment as soon as possible. He must be told of this, because other arrangements would have to be made. Scott felt that his usefulness in Tangier was over — before it had even started! But it was going to be tricky to contact Marchment now — tricky and dangerous. There was no doubt that his every movement was watched, and the only means he had of reaching Marchment was if he showed himself to Kettleby tomorrow morning in the Little Socco.

And he dare not do that!

The white-faced man's threat had been no idle one. If he, Scott, was not on the Lisbon plane leaving Tangier in the morning . . . ?

Egerton lit another cigarette, got up and poured out another John Haig. He drank a little, put down the glass, and started to pace up and down the room trying to find an answer to his problem.

It was after three o'clock in the morning before he found it.

6

I

In his dingy apartment over the wine shop, Marchment sat at his desk smoking a cigarette and drinking coffee. Over his small, beady eyes his brows were drawn down in a worried frown.

It was nearly eleven o'clock on the morning following Egerton Scott's visit from the white-faced man, and he was expecting the arrival of Kettleby. Marchment had heard all about the murder of Ogden at the old Hassan Tower, and that Scott had been questioned by the police. He had means by which such items of information reached him. Kettleby would bring him the latest news, culled from the gossip that ran through the Little Socco almost with the speed of an electric current. Nothing happened in Tangier that was not almost immediately known in the market places, passing rapidly from mouth to mouth — a grape vine that was more efficient than a telegraph system.

He had finished his coffee and started another cigarette, before Kettleby, shabby and shuffling as usual, came in.

'Well?' Marchment put the question as Kettleby threw his hat on a chair.

'I don't know that it is well.' Kettleby passed a none too clean hand over his thin bald head.

'Why, what's happened?' snapped Marchment sharply.

'Scott's vanished,' said Kettleby. He pulled up a chair and sat down wearily. 'I don't like the look of it at all . . . '

'What do you mean — vanished?' demanded Marchment.

'He left the Minezeh Hotel during the night,' said Kettleby, reaching over to the box on the desk and taking a cigarette. 'His bed hadn't been slept in . . . '

'Perhaps he didn't come back last night,' said Marchment, but his frown had deepened so that his eyes were almost invisible. 'There are lots of places in Tangier where he might have gone . . . '

'He came back just before midnight,'

broke in Kettleby. 'He got his key from the reception desk and went up to his room. But he wasn't there when his early tea was taken up, and, as I said, his bed hadn't been slept in . . . '

Marchment picked up a pencil, looked at it, and put it down again.

'Nobody saw him go out again,' went on Kettleby. 'His car's still there and so is his luggage . . . '

'How did you hear this?' asked Marchment.

'The whole of Tangier is buzzing with it,' said Kettleby. 'The general opinion is that he shot Ogden . . . '

'It would be,' said Marchment. He got up abruptly and began to pace about the room. 'I suppose the police had been notified?'

Kettleby nodded. He looked tired and haggard. There were dark smudges under his watery eyes.

'The manager of the hotel rang them up,' he said. 'It looks bad, doesn't it?'

'He may have had a good reason,' said Marchment. 'But I don't like it — I don't like it at all . . . '

Kettleby, who had been fiddling with the unlighted cigarette, fished a box of matches from the pocket of his soiled and crumpled jacket and struck one.

'D'you think they've got on to him?' he asked dipping the end of the cigarette in the flame and drawing in a lungful of smoke.

'That's what I'm afraid of,' said Marchment. 'But, of course, we've no proof. As I suggested, he may have had a good reason for disappearing suddenly, and there's nothing to show that he won't come back. After all, a man's entitled to absent himself from his hotel for a night or so, isn't he? The manager was a bit previous in informing the police . . . '

'I think he wanted to put himself on the right side,' said Kettleby. 'The police had been there questioning Scott about the Ogden business. The manager may have believed that he was mixed up in it.'

Marchment nodded absently. He was obviously worried over this new development.

'There's nothing much we can do,' he remarked. 'He can't very well contact us, even if he's in a position to,' he added meaningly. 'He doesn't know my address. The arrangement was to meet at the Hassan Tower, if he wanted to get in touch. He'd let you know by visiting the café in the Little Socco . . . '

'There's a chance that's what he'll do,' said Kettleby. 'I'll still keep the date every morning — just in case.' By his tone he didn't sound too hopeful.

Marchment sighed.

'I suppose we'd better let London know about it,' he said. 'They'll go right up in the air . . . Oh well, I don't see that we could help it! How the devil did they get on to him — that's what I'd like to know . . . '

'And how soon will it be before they get on to us?' grunted Kettleby.

'If they do that we shall know soon enough,' said Marchment.

II

In the strange-smelling labyrinth of the lower Kasbah, where it is possible to get completely lost quicker than in Hampton Court Maze, an Arab in a long soiled robe of striped cotton with a black and white *keffiyah* on his head, held in place by the black silk *agal*, moved slowly along the narrow street that was one of many similar streets crossing and intersecting. It is said that the Kasbah holds little harm. It is also said, with more truth, that its dimness and secrecy is a hiding place for all the scum and cut-throats of Tangier. Dim and narrow alleys run crookedly down beside towering house walls, and the lights, at night, are few and far between. The streets are full of the odours of Arab cooking — only those who have smelled it can realise how nauseous it can be — and foreign garbage.

At night the Kasbah is quiet, eerie and mysterious. No chink of light seeps out from the ghostly street doors of the houses, shut fast. Yet, all the time, there is a sense of furtive, unseen life moving in the shadows.

The Arab turned into a long, narrow street, inside high dirty white walls, then into another and another. He passed several other figures moving slowly in the other direction, but they took no notice of him. His like was too common a sight in the crooked byways of the Kasbah.

They would have been surprised if they had known that under that soiled robe and beneath the *keffiyah* was an Englishman.

This was the plan that had come to Egerton Scott in the small hours of the morning — the only way, so far as he could see, of eluding 'Group X.' Even when the idea entered his mind, he saw the difficulties it presented. First he had to get out of the hotel, and that was the easiest of his problems. The second, and infinitely more difficult, was procuring a disguise. There was nobody he could go to in Tangier. He thought of Marchment, but he didn't know where to find him, and he had to drop the character of Egerton Scott and assume his other character without delay. The hotel was most certainly watched and he couldn't afford to be seen in the streets.

He had a plan for getting out of the Minzeh, but what then? Where could he go? He knew sufficient about Tangier to realize that the Kasbah was his best bet. He could lose himself there without difficulty . . .

But he had to get there, *and* in a suitable disguise.

Jeanette!

If he could get to the girl's flat she might be able to help. But they would be watching that too, surely?

Watching for him . . . ?

He went over to the door and unlocked it. Opening it an inch, he listened.

Silence!

The hotel was sleeping. It was that hour when all activity ceased . . .

He peered out into the dimly lighted, carpeted corridor. There was nobody about, no sound except a faint and distant snore.

Gently he closed the door behind him, and walked softly towards where he knew the service stairs led up and down. They were of stone, devoid of covering. He paused and took off his shoes. Tying the laces together he hung them round his neck. He might need both his hands free.

On tiptoe, making no sound in his stockinged feet, he went cautiously down.

It seemed an age before he reached the kitchen quarters, a vast place and, as he had hoped, completely deserted. There was a single pilot light burning dimly in the ceiling which was sufficient to enable him to find his way about.

Now, if only his luck would hold . . .

He opened the first cupboard and found nothing but brooms and pails, dustpans, and a Hoover. The second was equally unproductive. It contained dusters, tins of furniture polish, brass polish, materials for shoe cleaning. On the floor lay a pair of very old brown shoes, cracked and falling to pieces.

He looked around. There was a door, partly open, on the other side of the kitchen and he went over to explore. It was a kind of scullery, but his heart leapt as he saw what was hanging up on a hook behind the door.

A soiled boiler suit!

It was the very thing! He had hoped to find some kind of overcoat belonging to one of the staff, but this was better.

This, with those old brown shoes . . .

He pulled on the boiler suit over his own. Fortunately it belonged to a big man and it wasn't difficult. When he had got it on he went over to a mirror on the wall and looked at the result. It made him look much bigger and stouter.

So far so good!

He put on the brown shoes. They were a tight fit and hurt him, but he managed it. Now, for the final touches and he would be away!

He felt like singing as he went over to the broom cupboard and selected a soft brush of black bristles. That would do! From the boot cleaning materials he took a brown polish and carefully smeared it over his face and hands until he had acquired a deep suntan. It wouldn't have passed muster in the daylight, but in the half-light, just before dawn, it ought to get by . . .

He rumpled up his hair, and then sought the final ingredient to complete his makeshift disguise. Some kind of adhesive . . .

And the only thing he could find was a

125

tin of treacle! Would it be sticky enough to hold?

He spread a little on his upper lip, found a knife, and cut off some hairs about an inch long from the brush. In front of the mirror he applied them one at a time to the treacle on his lip. They stuck!

When he had finished, his own personality had vanished! In its place was a rough-looking fellow in a dirty blue boiler suit, with a weather-tanned face and a scrubby black moustache. It was rough, and wouldn't stand looking at too closely, but there was a chance that it would pass!

He found the back door and cautiously turned the key and pulled back the bolts. He found himself in a small yard with a door in the wall. This was also locked, but the key was still in the lock on the inside. He opened it and looked out into a dim and narrow alley. At one end he could see the rue du Statut.

He was on the point of slipping out of the door when he caught sight of an old spade leaning against the side of a wooden shed.

He went over and picked it up. It would add an authentic touch to his disguise as well as providing a useful weapon, if necessary . . .

His heart was beating a little faster than usual as he slouched up the alley and turned into the rue du Statut.

Was he going to get away with it?

The street was deserted. He could see no sign of a watcher, but he was convinced that there was one somewhere. However, nobody challenged him as he slouched up the street, with the spade over his shoulder, in the direction of the rue Cintra.

Thank heaven, he thought, that Jeanette doesn't live very far away!

It was beginning to get light and there was still the gauntlet of the girl's flat to run. He had noticed, when he had taken her home on the previous night, that there was a small passage running down beside the souvenir shop. Passages of this sort are very common in Tangier. It would be better, if possible, to get to the flat from the rear. Perhaps there was a yard or something of the kind. At least, it was worth trying and would be less conspicuous than ringing the bell of the door beside the entrance to the souvenir shop.

He reached the place and, so far as he could judge, he had not been followed. He turned into the passage. On one side was the high wall of a house, pierced by windows that were now shuttered, but he breathed a prayer of thankfulness when he saw that the wall of Jeanette's side of the passage was fairly low.

But there was no door!

Scott couldn't hang about. If there *was* anyone watching here, it would be just bad luck. There was certainly no sign of anyone.

He leant the spade against the wall, using the loop of the wooden handle for a foot-rest, and managed to get a grip of the coping. A minute later he had hauled himself up and was astride.

The yard was full of empty packing cases, piled up one on top of the other, and he dropped silently down. He could see the windows of Jeanette's flat above him, but there was no means of reaching them. He could only hope that her bedroom was at the back. There was a window open which suggested that it might be.

He looked around for something with which to attract her attention, and discovered a long pole with a hook on one end, of the kind that is used for pulling down shop blinds or awnings. It should just reach the lower part of the window.

He had nearly picked it up when he realised what he looked like! If she saw him like that she'd probably be terrified out of her wits and scream.

It was light enough to see clearly now, and getting lighter every second!

He tore off the boiler suit and scrubbed at the sticky mess on his upper lip. He couldn't see the result, but he hoped that he looked more like himself. Then he raised the pole and tapped on the frame of the open window.

There was no result, and he wondered if she did after all sleep in the front of the flat. He tried again and this time he heard a startled exclamation. He decided to risk it, and whistled.

There was a pause and then Jeanette's head appeared at the window.

'Who is it? What do you want?' she asked in a scared voice.

'It's me,' said Scott urgently, 'Egerton Scott. I must see you at once. It's urgent!'

'Wait for a minute,' she called, 'and then come to the back door of the shop. I'll come down.'

Her head vanished from the window, and Scott went over and waited by a narrow door that was half-hidden by a pile of cases.

In a few minutes he heard the rattle of a bolt and the sound of a key turning in the lock. The door opened silently, and Jeanette appeared on the threshold.

'Come in,' she said.

He found himself in a small room behind the souvenir shop, with a curtained archway that led through into the main establishment. Jeanette, arrayed in a dressing gown, led the way across the shop to a door in the side-wall near the counter. This she opened and ushered Scott into a narrow passage with a staircase that led upward.

'Go upstairs,' she said. 'The door of my flat is open. I'll be up in a minute. I must lock and bolt the back door.'

She hurried away, and Scott mounted the semi-dark stair. The light was on in the girl's flat and he entered a large room that opened off a small hall. It was tastefully and comfortably furnished and there were several hats in various stages of construction on a large work table in the window.

He heard her lock the communicating door to the shop, and then her light footsteps as she ran up the stairs. The first thing she did when she saw him was to stare in astonishment and then burst out laughing!

'I expect I look very funny,' said Scott.

'You've no idea how funny!' she agreed 'What on earth have you been doing?'

'Trying to save my life,' he answered, and her laughter stopped abruptly.

'Do you mean that?' she asked. 'What happened?'

As briefly as possible he told her.

'I didn't want to involve you in this,' he ended, 'but I couldn't think of anybody I could go to . . . '

'Don't be silly,' she broke in. 'Of course, I'll do everything I can. It's lucky that the owner of the shop downstairs doesn't live in. It is also lucky that I have the key . . . ' She broke off and added quickly: 'I'll make some coffee. The bathroom is through there. You can wash the treacle off. You've got black hairs sticking all over your face!'

Even with hot water, he found it difficult to remove all traces of the shoe polish. But he looked and felt a great deal better when he returned to the sitting room.

Jeanette came in with the coffee. She had changed into a frock and tidied her hair. She nodded her approval as she saw the difference in his appearance.

'Now you are more like yourself,' she said, pouring out coffee and handing him a cup. 'It was a good thing that it was dark in the yard or I might not have let you in.'

She filled her own cup and perched herself on the arm of the settee.

'What are you going to do?' she asked, after sipping some of the hot coffee.

'That's where I want you to help me,' he answered. 'I've got to get a proper disguise before I can venture out . . . '

'You can stay here as long as you like,' she said. 'I can make you up a bed on the settee . . . '

'It's very sweet of you,' he said, 'but I can't do that. I must be able to get out. And apart from that, this is the first place they'll think of looking for me . . . '

She nodded.

'What do you want me to do?' she asked.

'Can you get hold of an Arab's robe?' he answered. 'The complete outfit? I think that would be the best disguise. There are so many of them in Tangier that another would only be like an extra pebble on Brighton beach.'

She finished her coffee, put down the cup, and rested her chin on one hand, frowning.

'You'd have to live somewhere, wouldn't you?' she said, after a pause. 'The safest place would be in the Kasbah. I know someone who keeps a carpet shop. I'll be quite candid with you. He's a thief, but my uncle was good to him once, and he will do anything I ask him. If I tell him that you are hiding from the police . . . '

'You can tell him anything you like,' said Scott. 'It seems just the right sort of hideout. But you'll have to be careful. I didn't *see* anyone watching this flat, although I looked very carefully this morning, but I should think they're certain to get around to it soon . . . '

'I'll be careful,' she said. She got up from the arm of the settee. 'I'll go and see Ali now. There is food in the larder if you feel hungry. I'll be back as soon as I can. If anybody comes to the door don't answer it. They'll think I'm out.'

When she had gone, Egerton Scott settled down to wait with as much patience as he could muster. Up to now, things had gone better than he had hoped. It would probably be some time before they discovered that he was no longer in the hotel, and by then he ought to be safely hidden away in the Kasbah.

Jeanette was a brick. He felt certain qualms at having dragged her into the affair, but she was really in it from the time she had gone to the Hassan Tower to meet poor Ogden. Certainly without her assistance he would have been in the soup. She had accepted the whole thing with a calmness and practicality that was amazing. A girl in a million!

There was one thing, he had plenty of money with him. Although he had been forced to leave his luggage behind, he carried his money in a belt next his skin. He had also brought his automatic away. That might prove useful if things got tough. Provided he could lose himself in the Arab disguise he was at a distinct advantage over the other side. They would be completely disconcerted, running round in circles wondering what had happened to him.

He found his way to the tiny kitchen and boiled himself a couple of eggs. These he carried back to the sitting room and ate with some rolls and butter, washing them down with the remains of the coffee which he heated up.

It seemed an age before Jeanette returned. She came in with a radiant smile, and he could tell before she said a word that she had been successful.

'I've got all the Arab things,' she announced triumphantly, 'and they're not new, but pretty old and grubby. They'll look more natural.'

'You really are a wonderful girl,' he said enthusiastically, and she coloured slightly at the warmth in his voice.

'I haven't brought them with me,' she went on rather quickly. 'Ali is sending them. If there is anyone watching, although I didn't see anyone, it will look better. I often have parcels delivered with hat materials. I've also got some make up and a false beard. You'll have to stay here until this afternoon. Ali is sending a covered van. The greatest danger will be when you slip across the pavement into it . . .'

'You seem to have thought of everything,' he remarked.

'I've told Ali that you will pay him well,' she said. 'He had heard that someone had been questioned by the police at the Minzeh, and he concluded that was you. I let him think so! As I told you, he's quite unscrupulous. I believe he dabbles in smuggling and all sorts of odd things.'

'I don't care what he does,' declared

Scott, 'so long as he helps me out of this jam.'

The parcel arrived about an hour later. It contained everything that was necessary to convert Egerton Scott into a rather seedy looking Arab with a straggling beard. The *keffiyah* concealed his hair. He took the whole outfit into the bathroom and emerged later to confront Jeanette.

'How do I look?' he asked.

'Horrible!' she declared. 'But nobody would recognize you!'

'That's the only thing that matters,' he answered. 'The beard tickles, and the whole get up is most uncomfortable, but I think I shall pass.'

'You can send me any message you wish by Ali,' she said. 'You must let me know how things are going. I shall worry.'

'Not so much as I shall worry about you,' he said. 'Do be careful. I feel very guilty at dragging you into this dangerous business.'

'I'm rather enjoying it,' she answered, and he knew that she meant it. 'You can't imagine how dull life can be at times.'

'When all this is over,' said Scott, 'I

hope we can brighten it up. Wouldn't you like to go back to England?'

Before she could reply there was a ring at the doorbell, and a disreputable looking Arab informed Jeanette that he had come for the 'goods.' At the same time he handed her a scrap of paper.

She glanced at it quickly.

'Oh yes, I see,' she said. 'Just a minute.'

She hurried away and presently came back with a huge roll of blankets that she had to drag along the floor behind her.

'What's that?' asked Scott.

'You are to help the man carry these down to the van,' explained Jeanette. 'It is Ali's idea. The van is drawn up close to the entrance. Nobody could tell whether one or two Arabs came in. These blankets will offer an excuse for *two* to carry them out between them.'

The blankets were rolled up. Scott took one end, the Arab, who had scarcely spoken at all, took the other. They carried them down the stairs to the front entrance. A small closed van was standing at the edge of the pavement, blocking anyone's view of the entrance. The doors were already open and Scott, at a sign from the Arab, lifted the blankets and threw them into the back of the van. He got up after them, the Arab shut the doors, mounted to the driving seat, and drove away at the usual reckless speed that everyone seemed to drive at in Tangier.

The carpet shop of Ali in the Kasbah was small and contained only a few rather moth-eaten carpets and rugs. Scott concluded that it merely served as a cloak that hid its owner's less respectable activities.

Ali was a little man of uncertain nationality. His thin, brown face was unprepossessing and he had a slight but decided squint. He welcomed Egerton without enthusiasm but was quite obviously willing to do anything he could as a favour to Jeanette. He made this quite clear. He provided Scott with a small room at the top of the house and asked no questions of any sort. In fact, he said very little beyond indicating that food would be supplied and that, apart from that, his visitor was free to do as he liked.

Remembering what Jeanette had said about money, Scott gave him fifty pounds

139

to be going on with and hinted at further remuneration if his stay was protracted.

Ali took the money and offered a word of advice.

'Nobody'll take any notice of you in the Kasbah,' he said, 'if you keep to yourself. You'll pass as an Arab so long as you keep your mouth shut.'

Scott kept to his room for the rest of the day but when darkness had fallen he decided to explore the Kasbah a little. It was all strange to him, and it might be useful to be able to find his way about.

He had been lucky. He had succeeded in getting away from the threatened danger, and the next step was to decide his next move.

Both 'Group X' and the Department would be very disconcerted over his unexpected disappearance . . .

III

The white-faced man who had given Egerton Scott the warning to leave Tangier, was speaking into a telephone in

140

a small room at the top of an old building in the Grand Socco.

'He's vanished. There's no trace of him at all.'

The voice at the other end of the wire was cold and unsympathetic.

'The hotel was watched?'

'Yes. We don't know how he managed to get away.'

'You have no idea where he has gone?'

'No. He didn't take his car . . . '

'Naturally. He isn't a fool, if you are.'

'He hasn't left Tangier. I'm sure of that . . . '

'He must be found. You understand? *He must be found.*'

'We are doing our best . . . '

'That doesn't appear to be very good — judging from what has happened. What about this girl?'

'Jeanette Dupris? He hasn't contacted her . . . '

'You are sure of that?'

'Yes, quite sure.'

'You have blundered badly. Everything possible must be done to find this man, you understand?'

'Of course . . . '

'He may try and contact the girl yet. Keep a close watch on her.'

'That is being done.'

'She might be the means of bringing him into the open. It depends. I will think about it and let you know. Don't ring me, I will ring you when I have made up my mind.'

'What about Kettleby?'

'That must be attended to.'

'You can leave it to me . . . '

'With more success, I hope, than you had with Scott.' The voice was hard, sarcastic. The white-faced man winced.

'It will be successful,' he said.

'I hope so. We do not like failures. That is all.'

The white-faced man put down the receiver. He took out a handkerchief and wiped the little beads of moisture from his forehead. He had never seen the man he had just been speaking to, he was only a telephone number that did not appear in any directory, but he was in deadly fear of that cold, inhuman voice. The penalty for failure was not a pleasant one.

IV

Sir Edward Fordyce looked across his desk at the Chief of Staff. His expression was a trifle weary.

'The dispatch from Marchment is worrying,' he said. 'Scott has completely disappeared. There seems to be no doubt that these people got on to him.'

'I can't imagine how,' said the Chief of Staff. 'Every precaution was taken . . . '

'There's a leakage somewhere — among our own organization,' interrupted Sir Edward. 'That's been obvious from the beginning. And the American side as well. They got on to Ogden. We didn't know anything about Ogden, but quite evidently he was an American agent, working on the same lines as we are. He's been — liquidated. Possibly poor Scott has too . . . '

'We've no evidence of that, sir,' said the Chief of Staff hopefully. 'Scott may have disappeared for reasons of his own. He's a pretty good man . . . '

'I know, I know,' broke in Sir Edward irritably. 'I shouldn't have chosen him for this job if he wasn't. But the best of men can fail. We're up against a very efficient organization. They've got *their* agents everywhere. In the most unexpected places . . . '

'The surprising thing,' remarked the Chief of Staff, 'is that they've managed to build up this vast organization without somebody giving *them* away . . . '

'In my opinion,' answered Sir Edward, 'nobody can.'

'I don't quite understand,' began the Chief of Staff.

'I don't think that the *central control* is known to any of the lesser fry,' explained Sir Edward. 'I imagine that there are several — how shall I put it? — rings. There's the centre, probably consisting of no more than a dozen people, perhaps less. Then there's an inner ring which receives its orders and passes them to an outer ring which in turn hands them down to the various isolated groups. And there's no direct contact with the central control at all. Even the inner ring doesn't know who they get their orders from . . . '

'It sounds rather complicated,' said the Chief of Staff.

'Not really,' said Sir Edward. 'Merely a sound piece of staff work, that's all.'

'And all this in aid of — what, sir?'

Sir Edward pursed his lips and shook his head.

'Ah,' he said. 'I wish I knew. Something very big. Something stupendous. Something that is obviously beyond politics and creeds and all the usual stuff. It's neither a capitalistic nor a communistic organization. Its ramifications extend through all countries . . . '

'A world-wide movement?' suggested the Chief of Staff. 'It might be a peace movement . . . '

'Could be,' agreed Sir Edward. 'Or a kind of gigantic 'Ban the Bomb' effort, eh? Whatever it is, there's a great deal of money behind it, and it's money that comes from *all* countries. Oh well,' he leaned back in his chair and passed a hand over his forehead, 'let's hope that Scott is still in the land of the living . . . '

'We haven't heard from the second string,' said the Chief of Staff.

'No,' agreed Sir Edward. 'There's still the second string. And if the first has

145

snapped, perhaps the second will prove stronger . . . '

V

A crowd of excited people of mixed nationalities swarmed round the harbour in Tangier. They shouted comments and questions to the group of uniformed police who clustered round something that had been pulled out of the water, and lay in a widening pool on the quay.

Most of the milling crowd recognized the soiled linen suit, sodden now with the sea water.

'Must have been drunk and fell in,' said someone. 'Used to drink like a fish . . . '

'A fish? That's good!' laughed his friend.

'He struck his head pretty badly,' remarked a third spectator. 'Smashed the skull . . . '

The crowd was pushed back by the police as a stretcher was brought and the body of Kettleby was laid on it and covered with a piece of tarpaulin.

The white-faced man had *not* failed to carry out his instructions.

146

7

I

News travels with great swiftness in
Tangier, and Egerton Scott heard about
the death of Kettleby very soon after the
body had been taken out of the harbour.
The news gave him something of a shock,
for it proved how well-informed these
people were.

He wondered whether they knew about
Marchment. Perhaps it was only Kettleby
they had got on to. The death was
generally taken to be an accident.
Kettleby had been seen in the Flamenco
Bar drinking his usual rum, and it seemed
to be taken for granted that he had
wandered near the quay in a drunken
condition, overbalanced and fallen into
the water, striking his head on one of the
piles. The police appeared to have
accepted this explanation as well, because
a wallet had been found in the inside

breast pocket of the dead man's jacket which contained two pounds. There was also some loose change in the trouser pocket. This ruled out the possibility of robbery.

But Scott knew that it was no accident, and Marchment would realize it too. Kettleby had been murdered and by the same people who had murdered Ogden and Magda. If he, Scott, hadn't been lucky enough to get away he would possibly have joined them.

There was probably consternation in the enemy's camp at the fact that he was at large somewhere, but, he thought ruefully, they needn't worry. He hadn't the tiniest clue that might give him a line to them.

He had heard nothing from Jeanette although he had managed to send a message via Ali that he was safe and sound. He wished that he could get in touch with Marchment but that wasn't possible, and would be definitely danger-ous if his real association with Kettleby and the Department was suspected. He would have to play a lone hand, and he hadn't a single useful card.

And then Fate took a hand and dealt him an ace.

II

Jeanette Dupris discovered, to her surprise, that since her meeting with Egerton Scott, life had acquired an entirely different outlook. She had been content to jog along fairly happily at her job of designing and making hats and, although there was nothing very exciting about her existence, indeed it was very dull at times, she found it quite pleasant.

All this had changed.

She was conscious of a restlessness, an inner dissatisfaction, that she had never experienced before. She continued to go about her business but she found that the zest of hat designing was gone. Whereas it had previously occupied the whole of her mind, it was now thrust into a corner of it, the main portion of her waking interest being concentrated on Egerton Scott.

She would have hotly denied, had she

been accused of the fact, that she was in love with the man who had come into her life under such dramatic circumstances, but this was no more than the truth.

After this exciting and glamorous interlude, short as it had been, life appeared drab and disappointing. And yet, she told herself, she might never see him again . . .

She was busy at her work table when the ring came at the door, and she put down the hat she had been trimming, got up, a little wearily, and went to see who it was.

Outside was the woman who had been dining at the Orange Orchid.

'You are Miss Dupris?' she asked in her harsh, strident voice. 'I am Lady Boynton-Smith! I'm told you make very good hats . . . '

'Will you please come in?' said Jeanette. She ushered the woman into the sitting room. Lady Boynton-Smith looked about her with an expression of disparagement.

'You haven't a very large establishment,' she remarked. 'Is this where you work?'

'I don't need anything larger,' answered

Jeanette. 'I only design and make hats to order.'

'You have none that I could try on?' said Lady Boynton-Smith. 'I really can't be expected to give an order unless I can see what I'm going to get.'

'I'm afraid,' said Jeanette, 'that I couldn't undertake any further orders in any case, at present . . . '

'But that's ridiculous,' declared Lady Boynton-Smith haughtily. 'Surely for an important customer . . . '

'All my customers are important,' broke in Jeanette.

'No doubt,' said the woman, 'but I hardly imagine that they are in the same class.'

She walked over and surveyed a partly finished hat on a small stand.

'This is quite passable,' she said condescendingly. 'I don't dislike it. A trifle more trimming round the front, perhaps . . . '

'I'm afraid that is already sold,' put in Jeanette quietly. She disliked the woman. Any more trimming on the hat, particularly where Lady Boynton-Smith had suggested, would have ruined it completely.

'Pity,' remarked that redoubtable lady. 'No reason why you shouldn't make a hat suitable for me, eh? Do you a lot of good, you know. Of course, I shouldn't have it if I didn't like it, but with that understanding . . . '

'I've already told you,' said Jeanette. 'That I am too busy to undertake any further orders.'

Lady Boynton-Smith shrugged her shoulders.

'But, of course, you weren't serious,' she said. 'By the way, weren't you dining at that place in the rue Waller the other night?'

Jeanette admitted that she was.

'Thought I saw you there,' went on Lady Boynton-Smith. 'Can't cook veal cutlets, and the service was shocking! I shan't go there again.'

The waiter, thought Jeanette, will probably be intensely relieved.

'There was a young man with you, wasn't there?' said Lady-Boynton-Smith casually. 'Good looking young feller, but he seems to have got himself into trouble with the police. Do you know him well?'

'I know very little about him,' replied the girl warily.

'Just as well,' remarked Lady Boynton-Smith. 'He appears to have got himself mixed up with the murder of some American. A lot of queer people come to Tangier, y'know.'

'They do, don't they?' said Jeanette.

Lady Boynton-Smith gave her a sharp glance, but the girl's face was innocent.

'Probably he was some kind of international crook,' remarked the woman. 'Anyway, he's disappeared from his hotel. I hear that the police are looking for him. Of course, if it was our police in England they'd never have let him get away, but these foreigners . . . ' She made an expressive gesture. 'Glad he wasn't a particular friend of yours.'

The woman was trying to pump her. This was the real reason for her visit. She wasn't interested in hats. She was interested in the whereabouts of Egerton Scott!

'He was a very casual acquaintance,' she said coolly. 'I am sorry that I cannot be of more help to you, Lady Boynton-Smith . . . '

'I'm sure you could, if you wanted to,' retorted the woman meaningly. 'Perhaps, I will come again when you are less busy. Good morning.'

She nodded curtly and walked to the door. Jeanette followed her and escorted her out.

When the woman had gone, the girl went back to her work table. But she couldn't concentrate on what she was doing. The visit of Lady Boynton-Smith had disturbed her. Was this high-handed, and altogether objectionable woman, one of the people who were after Egerton Scott?

It seemed hardly possible that a titled English woman could be mixed up with a group who didn't stick at murder if it suited them. And yet . . . ? Scott had said that there were people very high up concerned in the matter, whatever-it-was.

She decided that when next she was able to get a message to Scott she would tell about the visit of Lady Boynton-Smith.

III

The stroke of luck which Fate decided it was time to put into the hands of Egerton Scott was partly the result of an accident and partly due to that mysterious quality in everyone which is known as the subconscious.

This extremely active, but unpredictable, part of the human mind goes on working busily, without the knowledge of its possessor, until it has discovered a solution to any particular problem that has been troubling the conscious mind of the person concerned. The solution is then erupted into the conscious mind, ready made and complete.

Unfortunately, the subsconscious cannot be controlled. Sometimes it works swiftly. At others it is slow to achieve results. If it is given too much to do, it goes on strike and produces no results at all. Quite often some small thing will trigger it off. And it was a small thing that did so in the case of Egerton Scott.

It was in fact a box of matches.

He had run out of matches, and,

unable to light a cigarette, he went down to seek Ali in order to borrow a light. He found him in the carpet shop peering at the contents of a cardboard box which he hastily thrust out of sight at the approach of his lodger.

'Matches?' he said. 'Yes, I've got a box somewhere.'

He dived into the littered drawer of an old desk that stood at the back of the shop and presently brought forth the required object.

'There you are,' he said, and Scott thanked him and went back to his room.

He lit a cigarette and sat down on the edge of the bed, twisting the matchbox about in his fingers. It reminded him of the matchbox that had been found in the clenched hand of Magda; of the match-box he had found near the dead body of the American . . .

Two safety matches and three with red tips . . .

The box Ali had given him was a new box of safety matches. A well-known English brand . . . *A well-known English brand . . . !*

Bryant and May!

There was another brand, equally well known, a brand with red tips . . .

Swan!

And the whole thing clicked into place!

Alison Mae Swanson!

The 'Mae' was spelt differently, of course, and 'son' had been added to the 'swan,' but the picture was clear.

Alison Mae Swanson, the American millionairess!

Egerton Scott got to his feet and began to pace up and down the small room. His heart was beating excitedly. It *must* be right! It fitted so perfectly. The yacht would make a perfect headquarters — and that queer party of fabulously rich men of different nationalities . . . *The central control* . . .

The more he considered it the more certain he became. It just couldn't be a coincidence . . .

Scott wondered why he hadn't thought of it before. It was so obvious. But things worked like that. You missed the obvious until something shoved it under your nose . . .

And really, who would suspect these people of being other than they seemed? The answer to that was that no one had — with the exception of Magda, and possibly Ogden.

Magda must have discovered the significance of the matchbox . . .

Egerton Scott stubbed out his cigarette and lit another. At last he had got a break! There was still a great deal to do and he would have to go warily. There was no real proof that these people were the controlling factor of 'Group X.' Nor, as yet, had he any idea what lay behind that organization. But one thing seemed certain. It was not money. Unless the sum involved was so enormous as to be almost astronomical, these people were too rich to worry about acquiring more.

What, then, was their object?

Something that was so important that a few human lives were worth sacrificing in order to achieve it . . .

The secret lay on board the M.Y. *Cygnet*.

Somehow or other he must get on board that yacht. It shouldn't be difficult.

He was a good swimmer and the distance was not very far from the shore to where she lay at anchor.

But it would have to be done at night.

That meant he had all the rest of the day to make his plans. He would need a swim suit . . .

He went in search of Ali.

'Yes, that I can get for you,' said Ali, without evincing any surprise at the request. 'Anything can be got in Tangier for a price . . . '

'I am willing to pay you well,' said Scott, and added: 'Could you also obtain a small automatic pistol?'

'I have said that anything can be obtained in Tangier at a price,' rejoined Ali calmly. 'The pistol, it will cost a lot of English pounds . . . '

'I'll give you a hundred,' said Scott.

'For that,' replied Ali, 'I will see that the pistol is also loaded!'

8

I

The sky over Tangier was a deep blue. Myriads of stars twinkled like diamond points on velvet. The night was warm with scarcely a breeze to disturb the waters of the Mediterranean where they softly lapped the base of the square, stone tower that stood on the edge of the Kasbah. Beyond the great concrete mole of the harbour, the M.Y. *Cygnet* rode at anchor, her riding lights shining clearly through the semi-darkness.

There were few other lights on board, for the time was well past one o'clock in the morning. Two yellow port-holes sent faint gleams across the soft ripple of the water to show that someone was still wakeful.

Egerton Scott stood in a secluded corner of the quay and watched the lighted circles, waiting for them to go out. Beneath the soiled robe of his Arab disguise he was wearing nothing but a swim suit. Round his waist he carried the tiny automatic which, true to his promise, Ali had provided. It was enclosed in a waterproof pouch attached to a belt. When the time was ripe, all he had to do was to discard the robe and the *keffiyah*, and slip gently into the water.

The quay was deserted, although Tangier never fully sleeps. There were movements in the Little Socco, and along the side streets, groups of night-birds wending their way home, or out on some nefarious errand, workers from the bars and cafés, all kinds of people whose business or pleasure took them out at night.

It seemed a long time to the waiting and impatient Scott before the yellow circles of light finally went dark. He waited another ten minutes before he slipped off the Arab robe and removed the *keffiyah*, folded them up neatly and stowed them under an upturned boat. He hoped that he would be able to retrieve them before their discovery gave rise to speculation.

Slipping quietly over the edge of the quay he hung for a moment by his hands and then dropped gently into the water. It was not so warm as he had expected, but it wasn't cold. He struck out, swimming with long easy strokes in the direction of the yacht.

And it proved to be further than it looked. By the time he reached it, and caught the anchor chain, he was tired and breathless and the muscles of his legs and arms ached.

Clinging to the chain he allowed himself to rest and recover his breath before going any further. Then he let go and swam quietly round the ship. There might be an easier way on board than swarming up the anchor chain.

But there wasn't. The trim hull rose in graceful, clean lines above him, unmarred by even a hanging rope. It was the anchor chain or nothing.

He realised that it was going to be a tricky business. There was probably a look-out on board, and it was quite impossible to tell where he might be. If he happened to be in the vicinity of the bows and saw Scott's head rise over the side it would prove awkward.

But it was a risk that had to be taken.

Egerton Scott found that swarming up the chain was not as simple as he had expected. To start with it was slippery. It also sagged and tightened with the movement of the ship. Twice he slipped back into the water and prayed that the faint splash would not be heard.

But at last he managed to grab one of the stanchions of the rail and hauled himself up, dripping like a newly landed fish.

This was the moment of danger. But all was quiet. Nothing moved on the fore-deck, although he could see a dim light in the wheelhouse on the bridge.

He climbed over the rail and dropped flat on his chest on the deck. If there was anyone looking from the bridge he would be less conspicuous. For a moment he kept quite still, but nothing happened.

After a little while he began to wriggle cautiously forward towards midships. The ship was larger than it had looked from the shore and beautifully appointed. Everything was spotless, holystoned and polished.

He came to the dark mouth of a

companion-way with gleaming brass rails that caught and reflected the starlight. The steps were carpeted, and as he explored further, cut off at the bottom by a polished wood door that was shut. He paused and listened. There was still no sound. Probably the look-out was dozing. Was the companion-way door locked?

He tried the handle softly. It turned easily and the door opened. Actually it was two doors that opened in the middle. Scott stepped carefully into a carpeted corridor, wide and spacious. He could smell the perfume of flowers mingled with an expensive synthetic perfume that he didn't know the name of but associated with the owner, Alison Mae Swanson. It was the kind of exotic perfume that he imagined she would use.

Presently he came to the main saloon. It was large and luxuriously furnished. It was very dark and he couldn't see very well, but his sense of touch told him that the hangings and upholstery were of silk brocade. The smell of flowers was stronger here and he could dimly make out the huge bowls and vases filled with them.

Well, he had achieved his object. He had succeeded in getting on board. The next step was to find a suitable hiding place before the morning came.

He moved forward to a door at the further end of the saloon that he thought would lead to the rest of the ship. He had almost reached it when he heard a sound from behind it. Someone was coming!

He stepped quickly to a big settee that was set at an angle in one corner of the saloon, and dropped down behind it.

He wasn't a moment too soon, either, because the door opened and there was a click as the lights came on. They were subdued lights in silver wall-brackets with silk shades, but they clearly revealed Alison Mae Swanson as she came in.

She was fully dressed and she held in her hand a bundle of papers. These she laid on a side table and sat down in an easy chair beside it. There was a silver box of cigarettes on the table and she helped herself to one and lit it with a big silver table-lighter.

Scott watched her as she picked up the bundle of papers and began to sort through them. Obviously she had never been to bed, he thought. But he had seen no light when he had been swimming round the ship. She must have had the curtains drawn over the portholes of her cabin. It was a lucky thing that she hadn't entered the saloon earlier . . .

He watched her as she methodically sorted the papers on her lap and then began to read them one by one. They appeared to be letters or reports.

Sometimes, as she read, she nodded in approval, sometimes a slight frown wrinkled her smooth forehead. Scott would have given a good deal to get a glimpse of what she was reading so diligently. Probably it would have supplied him with the information he sought.

Perhaps there would be an opportunity . . .

A faint sound attracted his attention. It came from beyond the partly open door of the saloon, the door through which Alison Mae Swanson had entered.

The woman heard it too, for she looked up quickly. A man came into the saloon. He was wearing a dressing gown over pyjamas with a silk scarf knotted round his throat.

It was the tall American whom Ogden had pointed out at the Cosmo Club. Robert H. Glenn, the steel millionaire.

'I heard you pass my cabin door,' he said as he came in. 'I guess I couldn't sleep, either. You working, Alison?'

'I'm just going through these reports again,' answered the woman. 'They are fairly satisfactory.'

Glenn moved over to a chair near her and sat down.

'They are having trouble with the Soviet Leader,' he remarked. 'Didn't you say that?'

She nodded.

'Yes,' she replied. 'The English Prime Minister and the U.S. President are doing very well indeed — particularly the President.'

'They will have to do better than very well,' said Glenn. 'Nothing short of perfection will do.'

'There is time yet,' she said. 'Just over three months. They will have reached perfection by then.'

'I hope so,' said Glenn. He sighed. 'This is a tremendous task we have undertaken, Alison . . . '

'But the result will be worth it,' she broke in quickly. 'Worth all the time and trouble and money that has been lavished on the scheme . . . '

'And the lives that have been sacrificed?' he asked quietly.

'Yes,' she declared passionately. 'What do a few lives matter if this thing can be achieved?'

'They matter to the people concerned,' he answered.

She looked at him sharply.

'You are in a strange mood tonight, Robert,' she said. 'What is the matter with you? You have always been so enthusiastic . . . '

'Don't get me wrong,' he interrupted. 'I am still enthusiastic. But sometimes I wonder . . . Can we pull it off? Is such a colossal undertaking possible?'

'We have been successful up to now,' she retorted.

'Oh yes, I know,' he said. 'But compared with what we still have to do, it is a drop in the ocean.'

'We shall succeed,' she declared confidently. 'I am convinced that we shall succeed. Think, Robert, what it will mean. The end of fear! The world will no longer be living in the shadow of destruction! All the money that is now being poured into the discovery of better and more powerful methods of annihilation can be used for the benefit of mankind — for constructive purposes . . . '

'Will mankind be sufficiently sensible to take advantage of what we give it?' asked Glenn. 'For a time, perhaps, and then the race will start all over again . . . '

'It would have to start from the beginning,' she said, 'and by then there will be no need for countries to try and outdo each other in the possession of nuclear weapons. They will be under one Government — a World Government consisting of representatives from every country . . . '

Egerton Scott listened enthralled. So this was the object of the organization known as 'Group X?' But how did they hope to achieve it? What had Alison meant by her references to the Soviet Leader, the Prime Minister, and the President?

Glenn was speaking again.

'I guess, you make it sound good,' he remarked. 'And we've got an enormous number of people on our side. The danger will be that you cannot destroy memory as you can destroy material things. There will be scientists who *remember*. They will not have to start again from scratch. It will all be in their minds.'

'They will have to be dealt with as we have already dealt with the ones who would not listen to reason,' she replied. 'The majority, I am sure, will agree. They will be glad to turn their knowledge to something more worthwhile than the destruction of the world . . . '

'That is what I have never liked,' said Glenn, shaking his head. 'The necessity for — murder.'

'The sacrifice of the lesser for the greater good,' she said. 'If these weapons are allowed to go on, and there should be war, millions of innocent people would die, and die hideously! Don't forget that, and it is the argument that has got so many to join us. War is in the hands of a handful of men. It only needs the pressing of a button to release all its horrors. And these men would be safe! They would be in deep and specially prepared shelters while the holocaust raged above them! Isn't it better that a comparative few should die to save the lives of millions?'

The old argument, thought Scott. But who had the right to decide who should live and who should die? That was something that belonged to God. And yet, he admitted, that Alison Mae Swanson's argument was insidiously practical. It would have an immense appeal to the majority.

'We are not alone in thinking this way,' went on Mrs. Swanson. 'We have the co-operation of a vast number of people in all countries, including very many leading scientists. It is time that action should be taken to save the world before it is too late. The peoples of the world could have done it if they had all banded together in a vast brotherhood and refused to take part in this mad race for destruction; if they had said firmly: 'We will have no part in it. We refuse to help in the nuclear research laboratories, we refuse to have anything to do with the making of rockets, warheads, or any form of destructive weapon.' These things could not be made without the workers. But they needed leading. They couldn't do it on their own, or they *didn't* do it on their own. We have, I hope, supplied the leadership. Although we remain unknown to our followers, we plan and guide them. And we are guided by one who is a genius. Whose brain it was who first thought of this scheme and planned it.'

So these people were not at the head of the group, thought the listening Scott. There was somebody who was, apparently, in supreme control.

'I guess you're right as usual, Alison,' said Glenn. 'You must forgive me if I sound pessimistic at times. It's not that I'm not wholeheartedly with you in this. I am. I feel that it is the only way to avoid complete destruction of civilization; to ensure a future for the children who are now growing up . . . '

And at that moment disaster came to Egerton Scott!

It took the form of a small dog, a Pekinese, who came waddling in the door, snuffling through its pug nose.

'Dinky-do!' cried Alison Mae Swanson as she saw the animal. 'Come to mother, darling!'

But Dinky-do refused to 'come to mother.' Dinky-do was more interested in what the settee concealed. Sniffing and snorting, he thrust his head under the settee and began to bark loudly and excitedly.

Scott cursed silently. This was something he had not bargained for! It seemed impossible that he could avoid discovery.

'Be quiet, Dinky-do!' said his mistress severely.

But Dinky-do only yapped the louder and grew more and more excited.

'What's the matter with him?' said Alison Mae Swanson. 'There must be something in the corner . . . '

'What could there be?' asked Glenn. He got up and came over to the settee. Scott tried to wriggle further underneath, but to no avail. Glenn caught sight of him and uttered an exclamation.

'There's a man hiding behind here!' he cried, and with a jerk pulled the settee round so that Scott was fully revealed. Dinky-do, wild with delight, yapped and danced about madly.

'Who are you? What are you doing here?' demanded Glenn angrily.

'I ain't done no 'arm,' answered Scott in a nasal whine. 'Take that dawg away . . .'

Alison Mae Swanson came over and picked up Dinky-do, who was slobbering with eager anticipation of getting a sly nip at Scott's bare leg. He struggled violently in his mistress's arms, his eyes protruding so far that they almost popped out of his head.

'Be quiet, Dinky-do!' said his mistress severely. 'What did you come here for?' She looked at Scott coldly.

They *didn't* know who he was, he thought.

'I thought there might be some picken's,' he said in the same unpleasant whine. 'But I ain't taken nuthin'. Don't be too 'ard on me, lidy . . . '

'Get up!' ordered Glenn curtly, and Scott struggled to his feet. 'So you're a sneak-thief, eh? What shall we do with him, Alison? Have him locked up until the morning and then hand him over to the police?'

'We can't do that,' answered the woman quickly. 'He heard what we said . . . '

'Couldn't yer let me go?' pleaded Scott. 'I ain't done no 'arm . . . '

'Be quiet!' snapped Glenn. 'I see what you mean,' he added to Alison. 'What shall we do then?'

'There's only one thing we can do,' she replied meaningly, and Egerton Scott read his death sentence in her eyes.

9

I

Jeanette was worried.

She wanted to get a message through to Egerton Scott concerning the visit of Lady Boynton-Smith, but she dared not try and contact Ali. She had considered going to the Kasbah herself, but she knew that her flat was being watched and that she would be followed.

She might not have discovered that she was being kept under observation, if Scott's warning had not made her wary. The man who lingered at the street corner on the other side of the road with his tray of postcards for sale looked innocent enough, but he had never been there before and it was not the kind of site that a street vendor would choose.

She had put the matter to a test, which satisfied her that he was there for no other purpose than to spy on her movements.

She had gone out, walking rapidly to the Little Socco. Out of the corner of her eye she had seen the man with the tray give a signal to someone further up the street, and another man had followed her. She bought some ribbon at a stall in the market and returned home, the other man trailing her all the time.

Was the rear of the premises being watched too, she wondered? From the window of her bedroom she could see into the passage that ran by the small backyard. There was nobody in sight at first, but after a minute a man strolled slowly along the narrow passage, walked as far as the other end, turned, and came slowly back again.

The back was as well guarded as the front.

Jeanette went back to the sitting room, sat down, and tried to think what she could do.

Somehow or other, she must get in touch with Ali. The question was how?

For a long time she puzzled over this problem, but without finding any answer. And then the solution presented itself without any effort on her part.

There was a ring at the front door bell and when she answered it, Ali was standing on the threshold. He carried a small parcel, obviously to account for his presence to anyone who might be watching.

'You've brought a message?' asked Jeanette eagerly.

Ali shook his head.

'I have news, but it is not good,' he said. 'Take the parcel — it is only old newspapers . . . '

'What has happened?' she demanded.

'Your friend, he has gone,' said Ali. Briefly he explained. 'Where he went, I know not. But he has not come back.'

'A swimming costume and a pistol?' said Jeanette. 'What did he want the swimming costume for?'

'That I cannot say,' answered Ali. 'To swim in the sea, perhaps? But why, I do not know. I cannot stay,' he added. 'It does not take long to deliver a parcel . . . '

'This flat is being watched — back and front,' said Jeanette. 'I cannot go out without being followed . . . '

'It can be arranged,' interrupted Ali. 'In two hours' time come to my shop. You will not be followed . . . '

'You are sure?' she asked.

'I have said so,' he answered calmly. 'I go now. In two hours' time.'

He was gone before she could say anything further. She went back to the sitting room, frowning. Something must have happened to Scott. Or was he staying away of his own accord? Where could he have gone that required a swimming suit? Evidently something to do with the sea . . . A ship? Yes, but what ship? There were always a number of ships in Tangier harbour. Of course, at present, there was the yacht which had been there for several weeks, but surely that couldn't be his objective?

Jeanette, in common with the majority of Tangier, knew all about that floating palace and the people on board. A whole lot of rich people, millionaires it was reputed. Surely they couldn't be connected with the people Egerton Scott was after?

She gave it up and made herself some

tea. She knew that Ali would keep his word. In exactly two hours' time she could leave her flat in complete confidence that she would not be followed. She had no idea how Ali was going to achieve this, but she had complete confidence in him. Unscrupulous as he was in most things, so far as she was concerned he was utterly reliable. What service it was that her uncle had done him, she never discovered. Ali had never told her. But he had never forgotten it, and was prepared to do anything in his power to help her in any trouble. It was he who had found her the car to take her to Hassan Tower where she had first met Egerton Scott.

A glance from her window showed her that the man selling postcards was still at his post. Presumably, the other man was also somewhere close at hand. The watcher at the back, too, she discovered was still keeping his monotonous vigil.

As the time drew near for her to leave the flat she began to get excited. She had no idea what she was going to do when she reached the carpet shop in the

Kasbah, but this feeling of being a prisoner was getting on her nerves. There might, too, be some news of Scott, and it was the possibility of this that constituted her main object.

At exactly the time stipulated, she went down the stairs to the street. As she came out of the lower door, a van drew up further down the street, and three men got out. They started to walk up towards the seller of postcards. As soon as he spotted Jeanette he made a sign to the other man who began to move in her direction.

Jeanette stopped to look in a shop window. Out of the corner of her eye she saw two of the men from the van cross the road and stop talking on the pavement, directly in the path of the trailer. The other man went up to the postcard seller and started to look at his stock.

Jeanette began to walk down the street. The man who was trailing her followed. But he didn't get very far. An altercation broke out between the two men from the van. One aimed a blow at the other, missed, and caught the trailer on the side of the head. It was a heavy blow and he staggered. The next moment the three men were mixed up in a free for all!

Meanwhile, the postcard seller, seeing what was going on, tried to get away from the other man. But the man grabbed his tray and began to shout loudly, while the postcard seller argued violently and tried in vain to break away.

Jeanette would have dearly loved to stay and see how it all ended, but she decided that that would be stupid. She had her chance. The best thing she could do was to take it. So she hurried off down the street as quickly as she could, and made her way through a network of side streets to the Kasbah.

When she reached the carpet shop, Ali was waiting for her.

'So you are here,' he said. 'It has all gone as intended. You will not have been followed. You can go where you wish.'

She sat down on a chair to recover her breath. She had been almost running for most of the way.

'I don't know that I want to go anywhere,' she said.

Ali shrugged his shoulders.

'That is as you please,' he remarked. 'There is news of your friend . . . '

'What news? Tell me?' she said quickly. 'Have you heard from him?'

Ali shook his head.

'I regret — no,' he answered. 'But his clothes have been found. The Arab robe and the *keffiyah* in which he left here were found under a boat on the quay. The police are interested and very puzzled about them.'

Ali's unprepossessing face split into a lopsided smile.

'Then he must have gone into the sea,' she exclaimed.

'It would seem so,' agreed Ali. 'I cannot say. I only tell you what I know . . . '

'I hope nothing has happened to him,' she said. 'I don't know what to do . . . '

Ali remained silent, regarding her thoughtfully.

'You like this man?' he asked after a pause.

She nodded.

'You have not told me about him,' went on Ali. 'I do not understand what it is that he is doing. If I knew, it would be easier to offer advice, perhaps?'

She hesitated. Ought she to confide in Ali? Perhaps, Scott would be angry if she passed on to anyone what he had told her? It might spoil his plans. There was always the chance that he wasn't in any trouble . . . And yet, supposing he were? If she kept silent it might be too late to help him . . .

'Perhaps, he will come back or send a message,' she said doubtfully.

'Perhaps,' answered Ali. 'This man, this American who was shot, did your friend kill him?'

She shook her head.

'Then perhaps,' continued Ali, 'the one who shot the American would be desirous of shooting your friend?'

'There is more than one person involved, Ali,' she answered. 'I wish I could tell you, but . . . '

'You think your friend would not wish that I should know,' broke in Ali. 'I understand.'

'I don't know what to do,' confessed Jeanette. 'I don't know what to do . . . '

II

Egerton Scott was feeling much the same at that moment. He had been escorted to a small cabin, locked in, and warned that any attempt to break out would result in disaster to himself.

He had no illusions concerning his ultimate fate at the hands of Alison Mae Swanson and her confréres. He had heard too much for them to let him go, although they had no idea, as yet, who he really was.

He concluded that they were making up their minds just how he would die, and decided that he would probably be dropped overboard with sufficient weights attached to him to ensure that he would sink.

There was one consolation, if a very small one, and that was that his hunch had been right. These people on the M.Y. *Cygnet* formed the central control of the Group. So far, he had carried out his assignment successfully. Not only that, he had discovered what their object was. To a great extent he was in sympathy with them. It was time that something was done to ensure that trigger-happy governments should not be allowed to involve the entire human race in destruction. It was the methods that they were prepared to adopt, and had adopted, that he didn't agree with.

Nothing could justify murder, and these people had killed ruthlessly. They were prepared to go on doing this if by so doing they could achieve their object.

And they were not the entire control.

There was someone above them; someone whose mind had conceived this gigantic idea. This man, or was it a woman? was in supreme control. It was this unknown person who really directed the important operations.

The thing that had puzzled him, and still puzzled him, was Alison's reference to the Soviet Leader, the Prime Minister, and the President. What did that mean? She had said, 'The English Prime Minister and the U.S. President are doing very well indeed, particularly the President.'

At what were they doing so well?

Glenn had said that, 'they were having trouble with the Soviet Leader.' What kind of trouble? Above all, how did these men come into it? What part did they play in the scheme?

'They will have to do better than very well,' Glenn had said. 'Nothing short of perfection will do.' And the woman had replied: 'There is time yet. Just over three months. They will have reached perfection by then.'

Perfection in what?

What was going to happen in just over three months?

He gave up puzzling about it and began to concentrate on his own position. Was there any chance of escape? They hadn't troubled to search him, and he still had the small automatic, which Ali had got for him, in the waterproof bag under his swim-suit. Luckily the suit did not fit tightly or they couldn't have failed to see the slight bulge it made.

He took it out and examined it. It was quite dry and working perfectly. He pulled back the jacket so that a cartridge would be in the breech and put on the safety catch again. His swimming suit was almost dry by now, and he thrust the small pistol in the band at his waist where he could get at it easily.

It might be the means of saving his life . . .

He explored the little cabin. The porthole was screwed up tightly, but in any event it was too small for him to wriggle through. The door was fairly solid. He could have shot out the lock, but he concluded that it wouldn't do him much good if he did. The noise would bring someone at once and it would probably become a shooting match which he might, or might not, win. It would be better to hold his fire in reserve.

They were unaware that he was armed at present, and the element of surprise might prove to be a factor in his favour, later on.

The entire ship was very still. He could hear nothing except the slight sound of the sea as it lapped gently against the hull.

He sat down on the lower of the two bunks the cabin contained. It was nothing like so well appointed as what he had seen of the rest of the ship, and he concluded that it must be a cabin in the crew's quarters. This gave rise to the question as to whether the crew were in Alison Mae Swanson's confidence? It seemed likely that they must be. They had probably been very carefully picked and were, no doubt, paid well. He remembered the sailor who had directed him to the Flamenco Bar. He was part of the crew. If he saw Scott he would probably recognize him.

Which might be awkward . . .

He wished that he could get a message through to Marchment, but that was impossible. If anything happened to him, he would have liked to pass on all the information he had acquired to the Department . . .

But at the moment there was nothing he could do.

He would have to play it off the cuff. It was useless trying to plan ahead. This was a situation that depended on taking advantage of whatever was offered. Luck could decide one way or the other. In the meantime, he decided to take advantage of this lull in the proceedings and conserve his energy.

He stretched himself out on the bunk and fell asleep . . .

III

Lady Boynton-Smith strode with an air of great purpose through the Grand Socco, ignoring the importuning of the many vendors of merchandise, the entreaties of beggars, and the laden donkeys, with the same lofty disdain.

Although the day was hot, she wore a well-cut but rather shabby suit of tweeds and a hat of similar material with a feather in the band.

There was many a concealed smile as she passed, for reputations circulate rapidly in Tangier and Lady Boynton-Smith had become a subject of amusement in the markets and the shops.

Serenely unconscious of the impression she created and, it must be admitted, would not have cared in the least if she had been, Lady Boynton-Smith walked rapidly until she came to the quay. Here, she slowed down a little, peering out across the harbour at the smooth, blue water beyond the concrete mole.

A group of fishermen congregated round a bollard looked up as she approached them. Lady Boynton-Smith selected the more intelligent-looking among them and addressed herself to him.

'I want,' she said in her strident, authoritative voice, 'to hire a boat. Where can I hire one?'

The fisherman considered. Then he shook his head.

'No boats,' he said with admirable brevity.

'But, my good man,' remonstrated Lady Boynton-Smith, 'it must be possible to hire a boat somewhere?'

'No boats,' repeated the fisherman, continuing to shake his head.

'Possibly you don't understand me,' persisted Lady Boynton-Smith slowly, enunciating each word like a school teacher talking to a backward child. 'I wish to go for a trip in a boat on the sea.'

'No boats,' said the fisherman for the third time, and turned back to his mates who had been watching and listening with expressionless faces.

But Lady Boynton-Smith was not so easily deterred.

'I am quite sure,' she said, 'that there must be somebody who has a boat for hire. I have seen people rowing themselves about on the sea. Please inform me at once where I can get one.'

The fisherman shrugged his shoulders, but this time he said nothing.

Lady Boynton-Smith was vanquished. She gave all of them a glacial glare and walked away. The fishermen went on chattering among themselves in the same way that they had been when she had interrupted them.

At one end of the quay was a narrow flight of stone steps that led down to a small wooden landing stage. And moored to the landing stage were two boats, empty and with the oars lying in the bottoms.

Lady Boynton-Smith, reaching the top of the steps, and looking to see where they led, spotted the boats and her eyes glinted. She marched down the steps to the landing stage, untied the painter of one of the boats, got in, unshipped the oars, and calmly began to row herself across the harbour.

No one had apparently seen her go, for no alarm was raised. The owner of the boat was probably gossiping with his friends. Life moves very slowly in Tangier.

Lady Boynton-Smith's manipulation of the oars was rather uncertain. She dipped them unevenly with, in consequence a great deal of splashing. Her progress was slow but she managed to make progress.

Beyond the harbour the sea was a little choppy, but Lady Boynton-Smith stuck grimly to her task although the small boat was rocking as the waves slapped at its sides.

She seemed to find it difficult to keep a straight course, for she travelled in a series of erratic zigzags that were taking her in the direction of the M.Y. *Cygnet*. Two sailors, leaning against the rail, watched her with interest.

Although there was sufficient breeze to make the sea choppy, the sun was very hot and Lady Boynton-Smith, in her tweed suit was getting very hot too.

The perspiration ran down her thin cheeks and dewed her forehead. For a moment she rested on her oars but the current began to twist the boat round and she had to struggle at the oars to right it.

All might have been well if she hadn't decided to remove the tweed jacket. To do this she let go of one oar which slipped out of the rowlock and instantly drifted away. In her efforts to get it back she lost the other oar. The little boat swung round and began to drift broadside on towards the yacht.

Lady Boynton-Smith, in a panic, leaned over the side of the boat in a frantic effort to grab one of the oars.

And disaster overtook her!

She lost her balance, tried desperately to regain it, and fell out of the boat with a splash into the sea! It was soon evident that she couldn't swim! Floundering in the water like a playful seal, she grabbed the side of the boat and in her efforts to clamber back into it, succeeded in overturning it!

The interested sailors on board the yacht

saw what had happened and promptly took action.

They shouted to her to cling on to the upturned boat, an unnecessary suggestion since Lady Boynton-Smith was almost hugging the boat to her, and flung a lifebelt attached to a line as near to her as they could. It landed too far to be of the slightest use and they hauled it in again for a second attempt.

The boat, with the woman clinging to it, was drifting nearer to the yacht's side, and at the third attempt the lifebelt landed within her reach.

Following the sailors shouted instructions, Lady Boynton-Smith managed to grab the lifebelt and drag it over her head. The tweed hat with its feather had long since parted company with its owner and was bobbing along in the wake of the two oars. Gasping and spluttering, she got her arms through the lifebelt until it was round her thin chest with her arms resting on it.

'Hold on tightly, m'am,' shouted one of the sailors encouragingly, 'an' we'll pull you aboard.'

Lady Boynton-Smith hung on tightly. The line tautened and, with water pouring from her clothes, the bedraggled woman was hoisted up until the sailors, now joined by others, were able to grip her arms and pull her over the rail. She collapsed on the deck like a newly landed fish, gasping and trying to regain her breath.

'What's going on here?'

Alison Mae Swanson, immaculate in white, joined the group.

The sailors explained. Alison came over and looked down at the breathless woman. Lady Boynton-Smith tried to speak, gurgled, and swallowed with difficulty.

'Bring her below,' ordered Alison Mae Swanson.

Lady Boynton-Smith was lifted gently and carried to the companion-way. She was carried to a cabin and laid on a bunk, wet and dripping as she was. Alison followed, frowning slightly. By this time Lady Boynton-Smith had recovered sufficiently to be able to speak faintly.

'Terribly sorry,' she managed to gasp.

'I'm Lady Boynton-Smith . . . '

'I guess we'd better get you out of those wet clothes,' said Alison Mae Swanson practically. 'I'll send my maid with some dry things you can put on until your own are dry.'

'Very kind of you,' murmured Lady Boynton-Smith gratefully. 'Feel rather a fool . . . '

'Go and tell Louise to come here at once,' said Alison. 'And bring some brandy . . . '

The sailors departed.

'So very kind,' murmured Lady Boynton-Smith again.

Alison Mae Swanson said nothing. She just stood looking down at her unexpected guest . . .

IV

Lady Boynton-Smith, wrapped in a dressing gown over a suit of Alison's, sat on the settee in the big saloon. In an easy chair facing her sat her hostess, smoking a cigarette. Lady Boynton-Smith had just finished explaining how she had come to be in the predicament from which she had been rescued.

'Really, it was very stupid of me,' she said. 'I am rather fond of rowing and I thought the exercise would do me good. Can't think how I managed to lose those oars. Most grateful to you, Mrs. Swanson. 'Fraid I've put you to a great deal of trouble.'

'I guess we couldn't let you drown, Lady Boynton-Smith,' replied Alison. 'I hope you'll stay to lunch. After that, your own clothes should be dry and pressed, and I'll have you taken ashore.'

'It's extremely kind of you,' said Lady Boynton-Smith. 'I feel that I've put you to a lot of inconvenience.' Alison neither agreed nor denied this, and she went on: 'What a very lovely yacht this is. Are you on a long cruise?'

'It depends,' answered Alison. 'We go where we wish when we wish. We never make any plans ahead.'

'How delightful!' remarked Lady Boynton-Smith with a faint note of envy in her strident voice. 'You have a large party on board?'

'You will meet them at lunch,' said Alison shortly. 'You are on holiday in Tangier?'

'Yes,' said Lady Boynton-Smith. 'Never been before. Can't say I am very impressed. Too much noise and dirt!'

'Some of the surrounding countryside is quite lovely,' said Alison.

'You know it well?' said Lady Boynton-Smith.

'Yes. I have been here many times,' replied her hostess.

'Such a mixed lot of people,' said Lady Boynton-Smith. 'So many foreigners too.' The tone of her voice was completely disapproving.

'You dislike foreigners?' Alison raised her eyebrows. It struck her that if this woman disliked foreigners it was rather strange that she should have chosen Tangier for a holiday. 'I'm afraid that most of my guests are what you would call foreigners . . . '

'Of course, some are delightful,' broke in Lady Boynton-Smith hastily. 'It's all these Arabs and Portuguese . . . '

Alison smiled.

'I guess we haven't any Arabs or

Portuguese on board,' she said. 'We have a Russian and a German, quite charming men both of them . . . '

'Naturally,' said Lady Boynton-Smith. 'Of course, that is quite different! Not what I meant at all.'

Alison Mae Swanson rose gracefully to her feet. All her movements were smooth and rather catlike.

'I'm afraid you'll have to excuse me,' she said. 'I have some business to attend to.'

'Please don't worry about me,' said Lady Boynton-Smith, graciously.

'There are some magazines over there.' Her hostess pointed to a side table. 'If you'd care to look at them . . . '

'Thank you, but I lost my glasses in the sea,' answered Lady Boynton-Smith. 'I'm as blind as a bat without them.'

'I am sorry,' said Alison. 'Have you a spare pair at your hotel?'

'Unfortunately, no,' said Lady Boynton-Smith. 'I shall have to go to an oculist. Extremely trying, but it can't be helped.'

Alison agreed and left her.

Lady Boynton-Smith waited for a minute

or so and then she did a very peculiar thing. She opened the front of the dressing gown and pulled up the borrowed dress almost to her thigh, revealing a great deal of surprisingly shapely leg in the process. Strapped to her thigh with adhesive tape was a waterproof bag of oiled silk. She pulled it off, wincing at the pain, took out a tiny, flat automatic pistol and slipped it into the dressing gown pocket, together with the bag from which it had come. Then she rearranged her dress, pulled the dressing gown round her, and sat back with a sigh of relief.

V

Egerton Scott heard the commotion induced by Lady Boynton-Smith's aquatic act, and wondered what was going on. If he had had the slightest idea who was sitting in the saloon at that moment, he would have been extremely surprised. He would have been even more surprised if he could have witnessed the lady's actions with the pistol. They so nearly

201

resembled his own previous one that they might almost have been copied.

But he had no knowledge of Lady Boynton-Smith's presence on the yacht. He was far too interested in his own predicament.

The fact that he was still alive puzzled him. He had been confined in the little cabin all the previous day and night and had seen nobody at all, except for a husky member of the crew who had brought him food and coffee. This had reached him at irregular intervals, but no one else had come anywhere near him.

Still adopting the nasal whine, he had tried to get the man who brought the food to talk, but he, evidently acting under orders, retained a complete silence.

Scott had contemplated holding the man up with his automatic, but he decided that it was premature. It was doubtful if he would have got very far before being recaptured, and he didn't want to escape — yet!

There was not, at present, a jot of evidence against these people. They found an unknown man hiding in the ship's saloon and they were quite justified in locking him up. What he had overheard was only his word against theirs. And it could, with a little ingenuity, be explained away.

What he wanted was some kind of proof that the people on the yacht comprised the central control of 'Group X' and, also, proof of the objective that they were out to achieve.

And this brought him back to what he had heard concerning the heads of the three countries — Russia, England, and America. *What* was being planned? *What* was going to happen in a little over three months time? *What* were the three leaders going to do?

These people could not possibly have any pull over the Soviet Leader, the Prime Minister, and the President of the United States. That was absurd!

And yet they had talked as if they had!

Even if it meant risking his life, he *had* to try and find out more. And there was the unknown — the *real* head of the organization — to be found. It was probably due to this mysterious person that he, Scott, was still alive. Perhaps, he was the only one among them who pronounced the death sentence.

And yet, surely, they wouldn't bother this exalted being, who ruled people of the calibre of these ultra-rich members of society, about a little sneak-thief found hiding behind a settee in the saloon? Or *did* they know who he really was?

At any rate, thought Scott, a little grimly, I'm still alive! While there's life there's hope!

The thing that irked him most was the fact that he was without a cigarette. The craving for a smoke became so great that he determined to try and get one when next his food was brought to him.

He had no idea of telling the time — he wasn't wearing a watch — but he judged that it must be getting somewhere near the time for a visit. But it was quite a long time before he heard footsteps approaching the cabin door, and the rattle of a tray.

The key was turned in the lock and the door pushed open. And the sailor who carried in the tray was the man who had directed him to the Flamenco Bar!

His eyes widened as he saw Scott. He

stood balancing the tray on one huge hand and stared!

'Say, bud,' he exclaimed. 'I've seen you someplace before . . . '

'I ain't seen you before,' answered Scott nasally.

The man's face puckered up in an effort of memory.

'I've got it!' he said triumphantly. 'You're the guy who wanted ter find the Flamenco . . . '

'I don't know what yer talkin' abart,' grunted Scott. 'I never wanted ter find no Flamenco, or any other bloomin' bird!'

'I guess, you didn't talk like that,' said the sailor, setting down the tray on the bunk, 'but I'll take me oath yer the same guy . . . '

'Yer gettin' me mixed up with some other bloke,' said Scott. ''Ave yer got a fag on yer?'

The sailor produced a packet of Chesterfield cigarettes and held it out.

'Well, it's a mighty queer thing,' he said. 'I'll take a bet on it, bud, that you're the same guy.'

Scott took a cigarette from the pack

and asked for a light. The man produced a lighter and flicked it into flame.

'I can't figure this out,' he said, shaking his head. 'I've talked to yer twice . . . '

'Not me, you ain't,' asserted Scott, drawing in the smoke of the cigarette gratefully. 'It's me double . . . '

'Yeah, yer double-cross,' retorted the sailor, and went out, locking the door behind him, and leaving the pack of cigarettes.

Scott frowned. This was going to be awkward if the man reported the fact that he had seen Scott before. If they still believed that he was only a petty-thief it would rouse their suspicions. A thief was one thing — a spy was another! And after Magda, Ogden, and Kettleby, they would be more than ever on the alert.

He finished the cigarette and turned his attention to the food tray. It contained some chicken sandwiches, a slice of fruit pie, and a jug of iced water.

He was just starting on a sandwich when there came the sound of more footsteps outside, and the key turned in the lock.

This time it was Glenn who came in followed by the man whom Ogden had said was Montague Richards, the banker. Behind them was the sailor.

'This man says he has met you before,' Glenn began curtly. 'He asserts that your speech was different then . . . '

'I told 'im that he'd mistook me fer another feller,' broke in Scott. 'An' I'd like ter know 'ow long yer mean ter keep me locked up in 'ere? If yer ain't goin' ter let me go, why don't yer turn me over ter the p'lice . . . ?'

'Not so fast,' interposed Montague Richards in a deep and rather pleasant voice. 'I think we should inquire into your *bona fides* a little more, my friend . . . '

'I dunno what yer mean,' grunted Scott.

'I think you know very well,' retorted Richards calmly. 'Now, who are you, and what were you doing on this ship?'

''Ow many more times do I have ter tell yer?' demanded Scott. ''Strewth, if I'd known what I was fallin' inter . . . '

'You wouldn't be here,' put in Montague Richards drily. 'That's understandable!' He moved a little nearer to Scott. 'You know, my friend, I, also, believe that I've seen you before somewhere . . . '

Glenn looked at him quickly.

'Where?' he asked.

The banker shook his head.

'I'm not sure.' He frowned and pursed his lips. 'Wait — give me a minute.' His shrewd eyes ran searchingly over Scott's face. Suddenly he snapped his fingers. 'I've got it!' he exclaimed. 'The Cosmo Club . . . '

'The Cosmo Club?' repeated Glenn.

Richards nodded quickly.

'Yes, he was dining with the American, the night we were there . . . '

'Ogden?'

'Yes.'

Scott's heart sank. But he continued to put up a bluff.

'I look the sort o' bloke who'd eat at a posh place like the Cosmo, I don't think!' he said. 'What's the matter with all you lot? Yer seems to think that I'm a ruddy millionaire . . . '

'I'll tell you what I think,' snapped Richards. 'I think you're the man who disappeared from the Minzeh Hotel . . . '

'So it's the Minzeh 'Otel now?' sneered Scott. ''Strewth, I *do* get around, don't I? The Cosmo, the Minzeh . . . '

'We can soon make certain,' interrupted Richards. 'Get hold of Sneel. He'll know who this man is. If he's Scott, as I believe, the matter is serious.'

Glenn nodded, but his face was troubled.

'Come on,' said Richards. 'We'll wait for Sneel's confirmation.'

He went over to the door.

'Put a guard outside the door,' he said curtly. 'We can't afford to take chances.'

He went out, followed by Glenn and the sailor. The door was shut and the key snapped in the lock. Egerton Scott pursed his lips in a silent whistle.

Who was Sneel?

Into his mind came a picture of the white-faced man who had given him the warning at the Minzeh Hotel. Somehow, the name fitted . . .

10

I

Marchment turned into the wine shop, nodded to the man behind the counter, passed through the door at the back, and slowly ascended the stair to his apartment. He hung up his hat, locked the door, and sat down at his desk.

His round face looked a little drawn and there were lines of worry across his forehead. He helped himself to a cigarette and lit it, inhaling the smoke as if he found it soothing to his nerves.

The complete disappearance of Egerton Scott had rattled him considerably. More so than the murder of Kettleby. Things were going wrong. He felt uneasy. The warning light was glowing in his mind with a brightness that he couldn't ignore.

He, himself, might be in very grave danger . . .

What had happened to Scott? Where

was he? What was he doing? Marchment had notified London of his sudden disappearance, but no word had come from the Department as yet.

He wondered what he ought to do. It was useless just waiting for something to happen. At the same time what else *could* he do? If he acted, he might easily make the wrong move. Perhaps, they didn't suspect him yet.

He felt that unseen forces were gathering about him. Although he sensed danger, he had no idea from whence it would come . . .

He finished the cigarette and stubbed out the end in the ashtray. Getting up, he began to pace the room, his beady eyes half closed, his lips compressed.

If only he knew what had happened to Scott . . .

II

Lady Boynton-Smith, once more clad in her own tweed suit, which had been dried and pressed, sat at the dining table in the well-appointed room on board the yacht.

Alison Mae Swanson had introduced her to the rest of the party, and Lady Boynton-Smith found them a little dull. They all seemed to have something occupying their minds which rendered them silent and distrait.

The luncheon was excellent and beautifully served, but no one seemed to be very hungry. The women, not a very attractive lot, thought Lady Boynton-Smith, made a pretence of eating, but it was only a pretence. Only the German, Herr Graupner, did full justice to the food that was set before him. In complete silence, he worked his way steadily through every course, and even had a second helping of the mixed grill.

Alison Mae Swanson, at the head of the long table, did her best to make conversation. In this she was seconded by Montague Richards, but nobody returned the ball, so that, although several topics were started, they drifted up against a rock of monosyllables and were wrecked.

'We'll have coffee in the saloon,' announced Alison at last. 'I have ordered the launch to be lowered to take you back, Lady Boynton-Smith.'

'Most kind of you,' said Lady Boynton-Smith, as she followed her hostess to the saloon in company with the rest. 'I do feel that my stupid escapade has given you a great deal of trouble.'

'I guess, it was the least we could do,' murmured Alison.

Perhaps it is because their English is so bad, thought Lady Boynton-Smith, that they sound so preoccupied and stilted. But, of course, that doesn't apply to Mrs. Swanson, Mr. Glenn, and Mr. Richards.

With the exception of these latter three, they all made excuses after they had drunk their coffee and left the saloon. In a little while a sailor came to inform Alison that the launch was ready.

She led the way up to the deck, accompanied by Glenn and Richards. A long, low launch, very highly polished, with chromium fittings, rolled lazily at the foot of a gently sloping ladder set against the yacht's side.

'I hope you can manage,' said Alison Mae Swanson, as a stolid sailor helped

Lady Boynton-Smith through an open portion of the rail on to the top of the ladder.

'Thank you, yes,' said Lady Boynton-Smith, setting her feet gingerly on the ladder. 'And thank you once again for your hospitality.'

They watched her as she made her way down the ladder and was assisted into the launch by one of its crew of two. The engine started with a gentle purr, and the launch cast off. As it left the ship in a wide circle and headed for the shore, Lady Boynton-Smith waved.

'I wonder,' remarked Glenn, leaning on the rail, 'if she was genuine?'

'Surely, you don't imagine that she was anything else?' asked Alison.

Glenn shrugged his shoulders.

'I guess, I'm beginning to suspect everything and everybody,' he said. 'I've got a hunch that things are going to be mighty difficult . . .'

'That woman's genuine enough,' said Montague Richards. 'A typical example of the English County Breed, horse-face, tweeds, the lot!'

Which only goes to prove that even a clever banker can be mistaken.

III

Egerton Scott was lying on his bunk when the door was unlocked and Glenn and Richards came in. Behind them followed the white-faced man, looking as unpleasant as he had done at the Minzeh.

With his expressionless, dead eyes, he stared at Scott.

'That's him!' he announced, and the queer, hissing quality in his voice made the words curiously menacing.

'All right, Sneel. That's all I wanted to know,' said Richards. 'Mrs. Swanson will see you in her cabin.'

Sneel turned on his heel and went out. Glenn closed the door.

'I guess, you may as well come clean,' he said. 'Your name is Egerton Scott, and you're a Secret Service agent. Right?'

'We don't call it Secret Service,' said Egerton Scott in his natural voice. 'We call it British Security Service. Apart from that, you're right.'

'How did you get wise to us?' asked Glenn.

'That,' replied Scott calmly, 'is a trade secret . . . '

'Did the girl tell you anything?' interrupted Richards.

'What girl?' asked Scott.

The banker made an impatient gesture.

'You know very well,' he said curtly. 'Jeanette Dupris — the girl Ogden was going to meet at the Hassan Tower . . . '

'And was shot before he could do so,' retorted Egerton Scott. 'Which of your murderous bunch was responsible for that? The same fine Italian hand that shot Magda Vettrilli and bashed Kettleby's head in?'

'Answer my question,' snapped Richards, but Glenn's face was a little paler.

'Jeanette Dupris knows nothing,' said Scott. 'That's the absolute truth . . . '

'Then what made you suspect us?' persisted the banker.

'A little matchbox told me,' answered Scott. 'Whoever thought up that little gadget was just asking for trouble.'

'I always said it was a mistake . . . ' began Glenn, but Richards silenced him with a quick frown.

'I don't see how you connected the matchbox with us,' he said.

'Bryant and May — Swan Vestas — and it's as plain as a lighted cigar in the dark,' explained Scott. 'The matchbox was the great 'recognition signal,' wasn't it? Anybody belonging to your murderous outfit could recognize a fellow louse that way.'

'You don't understand,' muttered Glenn. 'Our aims are good . . . '

'But your methods stink!' broke in Scott. 'Well, I suppose I shall shortly join the rest of your victims?'

'That has to be decided,' said Richards.

'You heard enough while you were hidden in the saloon to know what we have set out to achieve,' put in Glenn. 'You are an intelligent man. Why don't you join us?'

'I'll admit,' said Scott candidly, 'that I am in complete sympathy with your objective. Who could help being? The fear of a total nuclear war has cast a blight over the whole world. The cost of research into bigger and better weapons is eating up money that could well be spent in something constructive for the better conditions of living. I agree that if this stultifying fear was removed it would be a wonderful thing. But I don't agree that this should be done by brute force! The cure is almost as bad as the disease.'

'We have had to take certain drastic action, I admit that,' said Glenn. 'People have been killed. But think how many *more* would be killed — *will* die, not only from the immediate effects of the bombs, but from the lingering effects of radioactive fall-out, if someone or other loses his head and touches the whole thing off . . . ?'

'Most people realize that,' began Scott.

'But they're not prepared to do anything about it,' broke in Montague Richards. 'They'll stick their heads in the sand and hope for the best, and they'll still be hoping for the best when the balloon goes up! We, and the organization under our control, are trying to make the future safe for humanity . . . '

'By murder, sabotage, and other dubious methods,' retorted Scott.

'Only those people who held key positions in nuclear physics and could jeopardize the success of our undertaking,' said Richards. 'We are not a gang of thugs! We are people who really feel very strongly about this thing, and who have dedicated their lives to it . . . '

'I appreciate your motives,' said Scott. 'But the kind of organization that you have brought into being is dangerous. It is as dangerous, in its way, as the thing it is trying to prevent. If it is allowed to grow, it will become unwieldy. Eventually, it will be uncontrollable — like any mob . . . '

'Before that can happen, and we have always been aware of such a danger,' said Glenn, 'our object should have been achieved . . . '

'How?' demanded Scott.

'That we can't tell you,' said Richards. 'But it does not involve violence — not, at least, of the kind you object to . . . '

'I'm afraid,' broke in Scott, and felt rather smug as he said it, 'that I'm bound to be against you on principle. If I wasn't,

I shouldn't be doing my duty . . . '

'To the State, or to humanity?' asked Glenn.

'To both, in the long run!' retorted Scott. 'You can't make these things work by *force*. They must come as a natural outcome . . . '

'I'm sorry that we don't see eye to eye on that,' interrupted Richards. He turned abruptly away and went over to the door. 'It is a great pity!'

He opened the door and went out. Glenn shook his head, rather sorrowfully, Scott thought, and followed him without another word. The key turned in the lock.

And that was that!

What would happen next? Scott had no illusions that he would be allowed to live. They dare not let him, knowing what he knew! And yet he couldn't help liking them — even respecting them!

They were so obviously sincere in what they were doing, devoted to what they considered was a great cause. There was no vestige of personal gain in the matter. They were all far too rich to worry about that, indeed, had probably spent a very great deal of money in promoting the organization.

But this might not apply to the lesser members. It was more than likely that the greater part of these merely had an eye to the main chance. That had always been the trouble with all 'great causes.'

The end of fear!

If this dream could be achieved what a wonderful thing it would be! But it couldn't be by 'Group X' or any other similar group. It could only come about by the wise and sensible approach, one to another, of the leaders of the countries concerned; by the elimination of suspicion and mistrust; by the working *together* for the good of all mankind . . .

Egerton Scott sighed.

It didn't look as if the future would worry him for very long!

But he still had his automatic!

He went over to the bunk and took it out from under the covering where he had hidden it. He must be careful to choose the right moment to use it. There would be no second choice . . . !

IV

Jeanette stared miserably out of the window of her flat on to the rue Cintra. The postcard seller had vanished and, so far as she could see, no one else had come to take his place. But she didn't care! Her visit to the carpet shop in the Kasbah had been a waste of time. She wondered why she had thought it would be anything else.

There had been no sign or word from Egerton Scott, although Ali had promised that he would let her know at once if he heard anything.

But the time went by and there was nothing.

All the same, she hadn't given up hope — not quite. There was still a chance that he was keeping away for reasons of his own. She tried to bolster up her waning hope with this, but she scarcely believed it.

She still hadn't confided in Ali. She couldn't bring herself to break the trust that Scott had put in her. But it worried her. Ought she to have told Ali? Would it help Scott? This question kept on repeating itself in her mind, but she couldn't find a satisfactory answer.

There was another question, too. Had Scott swum out to the yacht? Could that be where he had gone? It seemed incredible, but wasn't the whole thing incredible? Here she was, worrying about a man she hadn't known even existed a week ago!

She tried to tell herself what a fool she was; that this whole affair was none of her business.

But it was no good. Even if she never saw Scott again, life would never be *quite* the same . . .

She tried to occupy herself with her work, but her fingers shook and she couldn't use her needle properly. She decided she would make a cup of tea and went out into the small kitchen. She filled the electric kettle and switched it on. While she waited for it to boil, she lit a cigarette, hoping that it would steady her nerves . . .

And just as the kettle started to steam, the door bell rang!

Ali at last!

She flew along the hall to the front door and jerked it open.

But the person who stood on the step was not Ali!

'You!' exclaimed Jeanette breathlessly. 'What do you want . . . ?'

'Don't be alarmed,' said the visitor, pushing past her into the hall. 'I must speak to you. It's very important . . . '

'But . . . ' began the girl.

'Shut the door and I'll explain,' broke in the other quickly. 'Be quick, there's no time to waste . . . '

V

A dark sky hung over Tangier. There were no star points twinkling in the blackness tonight. Heavy clouds had come up with sunset, and a stiffish wind was blowing in from the sea.

It is not unusual for sudden storms to arise in the Straits of Gibraltar and they are sometimes very violent. No rain had, as yet fallen, but the smell of it was in the air.

The rue Statut was almost deserted. Not entirely, for three shadowy figures had congregated outside the wine shop, over which Marchment lived.

Two of them stood together on the pavement while the third entered the dark doorway. There was a short lapse of time, and then the figure in the doorway beckoned to the other two. They merged silently with the darker shadows of the entrance, and then were gone . . . softly, a door closed . . .

In his bedroom, with the curtains drawn over the small window, Marchment lay asleep. He slept quietly, breathing evenly, one arm flung outside the coverlet.

There was the faintest of faint 'clicks' from the locked door, and it opened slowly. The sound was not sufficient to disturb the sleeper, nor did the three figures who slid into the room like phantoms of the night, add to it.

'Do not move, or make a sound!' whispered a voice in the sleeping man's ear, and Marchment awoke with a start. A cold ring of metal pressed into his neck.

'The first movement will be your last!' hissed the whispering voice. 'Keep still! This pistol goes off very easily!'

'Who are you? What do you want?' muttered Marchment, staring up at the white blurr of the face that bent over him.

'Do not ask questions. Keep silent!' said the other, in the same hissing whisper.

Marchment lay rigid. You couldn't do very much with the barrel of a gun grinding into your windpipe!

The other two were moving silently about the room. Marchment heard the clink of metal, but he could see nothing for the body of the man bending over him blotted out his vision.

One of the shadowy visitants slipped out through the door and entered the sitting room. Going over to the large cupboard, a key was inserted in the lock, and the door was pulled open. The figure searched in the interior and found the steel cashbox. With a little murmur of satisfaction, the box was tucked under one arm, and the marauder went back to the bedroom.

'All is well!'

Marchment heard the whisper, and so did the man with the pistol. It was withdrawn sharply, but before Marchment could take advantage of this, the edge of the man's other hand came down with a quick cut on the side of his neck, and he lost consciousness . . .

Like ice before the sun, the shadowy visitors melted away. As silently as they had come, they passed down the stairs, through the wine shop, out into the rue Statut, and were lost in the darkness of the night . . .

11

I

With the exception of the man who brought his food, not his friend of the Flamenco Bar incident, but another, Egerton Scott was left alone. Nobody came near him.

He had asked for some cigarettes, and these had been sent in with his tray of food, so that, at least, he was afforded the solace of tobacco. They had also sent him a bathrobe to cover his nakedness, and the automatic now reposed in one of the pockets.

The time passed very slowly. More than once he was tempted to shoot out the lock and risk trying to make his escape from the yacht. But he held his hand. Prudence warned him that it would be a foolhardy thing to do, with precious little chance of being successful. The opportunity, if it came at all, was not yet.

Of the people who constituted the central control of 'Group X' he had only met Alison Mae Swanson, Glenn, and Montague Richards. He wondered what the others were like. There were, he knew, a German and a Russian. There were the womenfolk, too, of course, who had been present at the party in the Cosmo Club, but with the exception of Alison, he rather doubted whether they had much say in the matter. They looked the type who would do anything that their husbands told them without question.

Actually, then, the central control consisted of five persons, plus the unknown quantity referred to by Alison as 'a genius.' That made six . . .

Why, then, were there only *five* matches in the 'identification' box? The reason for the two safety and the three red-headed matches was obvious. It was an unlikely combination to get in a box by accident. *But why only five?*

And then he got it!

Of course, *the box itself represented the sixth person!*

It was symbolical of the position! The

directing brain that enclosed them all!

It threw quite an interesting sidelight on the unknown's personality, if it was the true explanation, for it suggested a colossal vanity!

It was dark outside by now, and judging from the motion of the ship, and the splashing of the sea against her sides, a rough night. He looked out through the tiny porthole but he could see nothing. The wind, however, sounded high.

He began to feel tired, and he must have dropped off to sleep, for he woke with a start to hear voices shouting, and a great deal of movement going on in the yacht.

Something had happened!

Scott had no idea of the actual time, but he imagined that it must be somewhere in the middle of the night.

What was going on?

He went over to the cabin door and listened. He could hear the faint sound of voices, among which he recognised Alison Mae Swanson's, but he couldn't distinguish what she was saying. But definitely some kind of excitement had broken out for the voices all seemed to be speaking together.

The yacht was rolling quite heavily at her moorings, and he could hear the whistle of the wind. It seemed to have developed into a stormy night!

The voices, and the sound of movement, died down and was followed by almost complete silence, except for the wind and the surging slapping of the sea against the hull of the ship.

Perhaps it was nothing after all. One of the crew taken ill, or met with an accident . . .

Scott switched on the light and lit a cigarette. His fingers touched the butt of the little weapon in his pocket, and the feel of it was comforting. He knew that he could never bring himself to use it against these people — they were, as Montague Richards had said 'not a gang of thugs,' but the threat of it might be sufficient.

The silence was broken by the sound of a door shutting somewhere, and then, after an interval, he heard someone outside the cabin!

Was this it? Had they decided that the

moment had come for his 'elimination'?

His fingers closed on the butt of the pistol . . .

The key turned in the lock, the door opened, and Marchment came in!

His fleshy face was pale and there were dark marks under his small eyes.

'Marchment!' exclaimed Scott in surprised delight. 'Am I glad to see you! How did you know I was here . . . ?'

'I didn't know you were here until a few minutes ago,' answered Marchment. 'I've been wondering *where* you were . . . '

'What put you on to these people?' asked Scott. 'They're the central control . . . '

'I know,' said Marchment.

He looked steadily at Scott, and suddenly Scott knew!

Marchment!

He was the unknown — the real head of 'Group X'!

Marchment saw that he realized the truth by the expression that came into his eyes.

'I tried to warn you,' he said. 'I sent Sneel . . . I didn't want to have to kill you — I dislike having to kill people . . . '

'Like Magda, Ogden, and Kettleby?' interrupted Egerton Scott. There was an icy edge to his voice.

'Yes. You don't believe that, do you? They found out too much. It *had* to be done . . .'

'At least they died loyal to their job,' said Scott, and Marchment winced at the contempt in his voice. 'No wonder there were leakages . . .'

'You despise me, don't you?' said Marchment. 'But you don't understand . . . I was trying to do something that was bigger than the Department . . .'

'That doesn't make you any less a traitor,' snapped Egerton Scott. 'You have been directly responsible for the death of people who trusted you — worked with you — looked upon you as one of themselves. Nothing can justify that . . .'

'I don't have to justify my actions to *you*!' said Marchment angrily, his face flushing. 'In my own opinion, what I did was its own justification. I've seen all the intrigue, and the lies, and the face-saving, that goes on among Governments. The organized mistrust, the prestige tricks, the vote-catching devices. You know them all as well as I do. The people of this world — the ordinary people who make up the vast majority of this benighted planet — are regimented into situations against their will, pushed into this and pushed into that, and half the time they don't understand what's really happening . . . '

'I grant all that,' began Scott, but Marchment held up his hand.

'Let me finish,' he said curtly. 'Without being consulted in any way, they could be pushed into war — a war that would lack all the glamour and 'glorious Technicolor' of previous wars — though, God knows, all war is hideous! The world has fought two wars to end all war, and the men and women who believed that are rotting in their graves! They sacrificed their lives to make the world a safe place for their children and those who were left. They believed all the slogans invented by the politicians. But the world isn't safe! The danger of war is looming up again, but a war, this time, so horrible, so utterly devastating, that the imagination reels at its dreadful effects. *That* was what I was determined to prevent. That's what I believe I *could* have prevented . . . '

'I doubt it,' said Scott.

Marchment shrugged his broad shoulders wearily.

'I shall never know, now,' he answered.

Scott looked at him sharply.

'What do you mean?' he asked.

'Because 'Group X' is finished,' said Marchment. 'Earlier tonight my apartment was broken into and a steel box was taken. It contained, amongst other things, a quantity of documents relating to 'Group X.' There was enough evidence in there to put an end to all our activities . . . '

'Who did this?' asked Scott.

Marchment shook his head.

'I don't know,' he said. 'But it means finish. The full details of the master plan were in that box . . . '

'What,' asked Scott, 'do you intend to do?'

'The ship is preparing to put to sea,' answered Marchment. 'I have spoken to the others. You will be put ashore before it leaves. You're not a danger any more . . . '

Scott laughed. It was a rather harsh laugh, with little mirth in it.

'What are you laughing at?' asked Marchment.

'It struck me what a fantastic ending this is,' said Egerton Scott. 'I am assigned by the Department to discover 'Group X.' I've done so. And now, although I'm a prisoner of that organization, I'm being put ashore!'

'There'd be no point in doing anything else,' said Marchment. 'I'll tell you quite frankly, that if your death would save the situation, you'd die.'

Egerton Scott took the automatic from his pocket.

'I suppose I shan't need that now?' he remarked.

'Didn't they search you?' said Marchment. 'That was careless. No, you won't need that.'

'What do the others think?' asked Scott. 'It's not much use running away, is it? They can be easily found . . .'

'I doubt if any action will be taken against them,' said Marchment. 'The Government wouldn't risk it. These people are too well-known, far too influential. It would upset the money markets of the world! The organization has been broken up. That's all that will worry the powers that be. The whole thing will be hushed up . . . '

'What about you?'

Marchment hunched his shoulders.

'I don't mind very much what happens to me,' he said, and Scott knew that he meant it. 'The thing I dreamed and worked for has collapsed in ruins on me. That's life, I suppose! Let's go along to the saloon.'

Only Alison Mae Swanson, Glenn, and Richards were in the saloon. Their faces were expressionless, although the shock they had received must have been a very severe one. Where the rest of the party were, Scott had no idea. He could hear a great deal of activity going on, and concluded that this was in preparation for the yacht's departure.

'Well, I guess, we're to part company, Mr. Scott,' remarked Glenn without emotion. 'The sea is a little rough, but you ought to make it.'

'I'll say the sea's rough,' said Alison. 'They're having difficulty with the launch. I'm sorry that we had to treat you as we did, Mr. Scott.'

It was all unreal, thought Scott. They were behaving like any well-bred people saying goodbye to a visitor would behave. But he admired their courage. The happening of the night must have been a knock-out blow. All they had planned and hoped for, swept away in a few short minutes. Years of work and money gone for nothing!

Something of what he was thinking must have shown in his face for Montague Richards remarked, quietly:

'Yes, it's been unfortunate. But even gilt-edged gambles fail at times.'

'I am sorry,' said Alison Mae Swanson, 'that we can't offer you some clothes to go in, Mr. Scott. I guess you'll just have to put up with your swim suit.'

'Well, that's all I came in,' said Scott.

'A good, stiff scotch may help,' said Glenn, and went over to a cocktail cabinet . . .

It was a tricky business climbing down

the slippery ladder to the heaving launch, but Scott managed it. The wind was increasing in violence, driving before it a deluge of rain. A swimming costume is the most suitable attire for a night like this, thought Scott, as he scrambled down into the launch, which three sailors, in streaming oilskins, were fending off with difficulty from the hull of the yacht. Blearily, through the curtains of rain, he could see the lights of Tangier, as the launch, pitching heavily, left the ship's side and rounded her prow.

This rather strange adventure was practically over, he thought, as he sat shivering in the well of the launch. There was nothing much left now but to report back to London. He expected that he would be reprimanded by Sir Edward Fordyce for leaving the job half-finished. That meticulous man would undoubtedly demand to know why he hadn't secured proofs of Marchment's complicity in the affair. But the proofs had been in the steel box which had been stolen from Marchment's apartment.

Who by?

That was rather puzzling. Marchment obviously didn't think it was an ordinary thief, or he wouldn't have been so sure that everything was over. He had been certain that the papers in the box had fallen into the hands of somebody who would understand their significance. Who?

Any further speculation on the subject was cut short as the launch began to make its final run for the quayside. It was by no means an easy matter to bring her in alongside, for, even in the comparative shelter of the harbour, the waves were dashing violently against the landing-stage in a smother of spume and spray. But the man at the helm managed it. With the skill of experienced seamanship, he eased her alongside until the rest of the small crew were able to get a hold with their grappling hooks.

Egerton Scott jumped across the intervening space, and almost fell on the slippery staging, but he managed to retain his balance.

The launch was away again at once, heading back for the yacht, whose lights showed dimly through the murk.

'Now what?' said Scott to himself as the rain splashed round him. 'Where do I go from here?'

The Minzeh Hotel was out of the question. There would be far too many awkward explanations to make. The obvious answer was Ali's carpet shop in the Kasbah. It was a good thing that the night was stormy. Nobody would be about to see him. Even in Tangier, the sight of a man walking through the streets, clad only in a swimming suit, was likely to cause a certain amount of surprised speculation!

He set off through the driving rain towards his destination, and in a short while was among the smells, and the labyrinth, of the dimly lighted Kasbah.

When he reached Ali's shop, there was no light to be seen of any sort, but that meant nothing. The inhabitants of that district hermetically seal their houses at nightfall, except for the places of ill-fame.

Dripping with water, his hair hanging in streaks over his forehead, Egerton Scott knocked loudly on the door. He expected to have to knock several times, but, to his surprise, the door was opened almost at once by Ali, himself.

'So you have returned?' greeted Ali without any vestige of surprise. 'It is well! Come inside, please.'

Scott followed him through the dark carpet shop to the room at the back, where a light was burning. The light came from a lantern, hanging from the ceiling, and shedding a pool of light down on to a table in the centre of the room. On the table was a steel box, like a large cashbox, the lid wrenched from its hinges. But it is doubtful if Egerton Scott even saw the box in the shock he received when he caught sight of the two people who were seated on either side of the table.

One was Jeanette, the other was Lady Boynton-Smith!

12

I

Egerton Scott's astonishment was shared by the other two. Jeanette, her eyes wide, stared at him as if he had been ghost. Then she jumped quickly to her feet.

'It's you!' she gasped, breathlessly. 'It's *you* . . . '

'Yes, it's me,' admitted Scott ungrammatically. 'I never expected to find you here . . . '

'Or me?' put in Lady Boynton-Smith, with a smile.

'Certainly not *you*,' agreed Scott.

'You've come from the yacht, I suppose,' said Lady Boynton-Smith, nodding. 'You must have been there when I did my film act and 'accidentally' fell in the sea. H'm! I didn't know that . . . '

'Look here,' broke in Scott. 'Who *are* you? You're not Lady Boynton-Smith! I happen to know her . . . '

243

Ali, who had disappeared, came quietly back and enveloped the dripping Scott in a large bathrobe.

'That's one of those things one can't foresee,' remarked Lady Boynton-Smith shaking her head. 'They're always happening . . . '

'Perhaps you'll do a little explaining,' suggested Scott, pulling the robe round him. 'Who are you?'

'I'm known to the Department as 'N.7.' My real name is Julia Price,' she answered.

'The Department!' exclaimed Scott. 'You're one of us?'

She nodded.

Scott looked at the shattered box on the table.

'Did you, by any chance, commit a burglary tonight?' he said.

Again she nodded.

'Yes — with the assistance of our good friend, here.' She indicated Ali, who bowed his head. 'He, and one of his friends, did all the hard work.'

Ali grinned his lopsided smile.

'I only do what Jeanette ask me,' he said.

Scott looked at Jeanette.

'You're in this as well, are you?'

She smiled at him.

'Miss Price came to me and explained who she was,' she said. 'She wanted to get hold of some papers which she thought might be in the possession of a man called Marchment . . .'

'I had to satisfy her that I was genuine,' put in Julia Price. 'I knew that she had helped you, so she must be all right . . .'

'So I asked Ali and he arranged everything,' said Jeanette. 'I waited here for them . . .'

'There is enough evidence in that box,' said Julia Price, triumphantly, 'to put an end to the activities of 'Group X' for good . . .'

'They've put an end to themselves,' said Scott. He explained what had happened on board the yacht that night. 'If it's decided to take any action against them, they can easily be found,' he continued. 'Personally, I believe that the Government will try and hush the whole thing up. The whole organization will collapse now . . .'

'Do you know what they were planning to do?' asked Julia Price. 'It's all there

245

— in detail — the entire plot . . . '

'There are two things I'd like to know,' he went on. 'First, what made you suspect Alison Mae Swanson?'

'It was through poor Kettleby,' she answered. 'It was quite accidental. I discovered that he was making discreet inquiries about the people on board the M.Y. *Cygnet* . . . '

'And that's why he died!' interrupted Scott grimly. 'Which brings me to my second question: Why are you here at all? I thought I was the person delegated for the job?'

'Well,' she looked a little embarrassed, 'of course, you were, but . . . I think I'd better let Sir Edward explain . . . '

'I don't mind telling you,' said Egerton Scott, 'that he's going to have to do a hell of a lot of explaining!'

II

Three days later, he was sitting facing the Director-General of the British Security Service in the latter's office in London.

He had arrived from Tangier, via Lisbon and New York, earlier that day.

'The whole plan was mine,' said Sir Richard, a little complacently. 'You see we had our suspicions of Marchment. There had, as you know, been leakages . . . '

'But why couldn't you have told me that you suspected Marchment?' asked Scott, not unreasonably.

'Because you might have given the fact away,' explained Sir Edward. 'A look, a word, an action . . . Marchment was a very clever man. My idea was this: he'd contact you, knowing that you were from the Department, and he'd make it his business to know *exactly* where you were and what you were doing. If he was up to anything, he'd see that you were safely somewhere else at the time. But, with Julia Price, it was different. He wouldn't know anything about *her*. She was free to go, and do, what she pleased. He'd have no idea that she was anything to do with the Department. We've never used her openly. She's always been an 'under cover' operative, even among our own people.'

'I was suspicious of her from the start,'

said Scott. 'But not in the right way. I thought she was connected with 'Group X.' You see, I know the real Lady Boynton-Smith.'

'Yes, that was unfortunate,' said Sir Edward. 'Well, things have turned out all right, eh?' He tapped a bulky file in front of him. 'We've got enough to round up all the smaller fry . . . '

'Are you taking any action over central control?' asked Scott. Sir Edward pursed his lips.

'That's not a matter for us to decide,' he answered. 'That's for the Government to say when they get our report. I rather imagine that these people's connection with 'Group X' will be hushed up. The whole thing has been kept very quiet, you know. 'Group X' has never actually become public. We were anxious to avoid that all along. Now that Marchment's dead . . . '

'Dead!' exclaimed Scott.

Sir Edward nodded.

'His body was washed ashore at Tangier, this afternoon,' he said. 'We had the news about an hour ago. Suicide, I expect. Jumped overboard from the yacht . . . '

'It's the best thing, I suppose,' commented Scott. 'That scheme of his was brilliant . . . '

'I doubt if it would have worked,' said Sir Edward, shaking his head. 'Do you imagine for one moment that these men, however cleverly they were rehearsed and coached in their parts, *could* have passed themselves off as the Soviet Leader, the Prime Minister, and the President of the United States?'

'I don't know. According to Marchment's written details of the plan,' said Scott, 'they were perfect doubles of the men they were to impersonate. The substitution wouldn't have been difficult with two of the security guards on the staff of each in their pay.'

'It was the most audacious scheme I've ever heard!' declared Sir Edward. 'To kidnap the Soviet Leader, the Prime Minister, and the President of the United States and substitute their own men at this Summit Conference! Nobody knew anything about the Summit Conference. Not even this Department! It was kept a closely guarded secret by all the parties concerned! It was to be a private affair, no publicity, nothing given out, until it was over . . . '

'And then the rejoicing world would have learned that not only were *all* nuclear weapons to be banned under a three-power pact, but *all* existing weapons, warheads, bombs, the lot, were to be rendered harmless and destroyed! It was a colossal idea!'

'But it wouldn't have worked,' said Sir Edward, shaking his head. 'Those three imposters couldn't have *stayed* in their parts, you know. And what would have happened then . . . ?'

'Would the *real* leaders have refuted the pact?' asked Scott. 'Would they have *dared* to refute it? That's what Marchment was counting on. In face of public opinion would they have *dared*?'

'That we shall never know,' said Sir Edward.

III

Over Tangier there was a full moon. It rode high in an arch of clear blue, deep and cloudless. The gentle waters of the Mediterranean sparkled with silver, a widening swathe that rippled softly.

At the top of a high, square tower, near the orange garden, that overlooked the harbour, Egerton Scott and Jeanette sat on either side of a small round table, on which were two glasses of hot mint tea, heavily sweetened. The only light came from the moon and a Moorish lantern that hung in the arch of the stairs. The murmur of Tangier came up through the still air, mercifully muted by distance.

It was nearly ten-thirty and there were no other customers for mint tea on the tower.

'I didn't think you'd really come back,' said Jeanette.

'I told you I would,' answered Scott.

'But I didn't think you meant it.'

She looked at him gravely, her dark eyes wide and serious. She wore a white pullover with a blue pleated skirt, and her hair hung loose on either side of her face. Suddenly, the sides of her mouth dimpled, and she laughed.

'What's the joke?' he asked.

'I was thinking of how you looked when you woke me up that night from the yard at the back of the shop,' she said. 'I've never seen anything quite so funny . . .'

'I didn't feel very funny,' he said.

'No,' she was serious again. 'Poor Magda? Did you find out what that list of girls' names meant? Did it mean anything?'

'Oh, yes, it meant quite a lot,' he answered. 'It was a code, invented by Marchment. Each different name meant a complete sentence. For instance, 'Vera' meant 'Instructions successfully carried out' and so on. It was the way Marchment communicated with the head of each separate unit of the organization, and they with him, through a central clearing house, in charge of Sneel.'

'He was a very clever man,' she said.

'Marchment? Yes. And really sincere in his belief that what he was doing was right. They *all* were. The way the organization was built up amounted to genius. They had their followers everywhere. Some of them with the same genuine belief as themselves. That's how they learned of the Summit Meeting, which was such a closely guarded secret that even the Department didn't know. It was to take place on a small island in the Atlantic. The island belonged to Robert H. Glenn, though nobody was aware that he was the actual owner. The substitution of their men for the three leaders would have taken place there . . . '

'Will the meeting still take place?' she asked.

'Yes, I believe so,' he replied. 'But a different venue will be chosen, of course. The organization is broken up, but they won't take any risks.'

'So many people died — for nothing,' she said.

'That always happens in any crusade, and this was a kind of crusade, wasn't it?' He took out his cigarette case, offered her a cigarette, and took one himself. He lighted them both. 'The worst thing that ever happened in this old world,' he continued, 'was the discovery of nuclear fission! It has changed everything, and unfortunately there is no going back. We can't! The knowledge is here to stay . . . '

'It could be used for a useful purpose, surely?' she said.

'Let's hope so,' he replied. 'Perhaps sense will come before it's too late. Progress hasn't brought much, only fear and an increasing tempo to life in general. Sometimes, I almost wish we could go back — to the peaceful and leisurely days of our grandparents . . . '

She took a sip of mint tea.

'What's your next assignment?' she asked.

'There won't be another,' he answered. 'I've resigned from the Department. It's no life for a married man!'

Jeanette dropped her cigarette and it hit the floor of the tower with a little shower of sparks.

'I — you — you never told me you were married!' she stammered.

'I'm not — yet!' said Egerton Scott. 'But I'm going to be! That's what I came to Tangier to tell you . . . '

THE END

We do hope that you have enjoyed reading this large print book.

Did you know that all of our titles are available for purchase?

We publish a wide range of high quality large print books including:

Romances, Mysteries, Classics
General Fiction
Non Fiction and Westerns

Special interest titles available in large print are:

The Little Oxford Dictionary
Music Book, Song Book
Hymn Book, Service Book

Also available from us courtesy of Oxford University Press:

Young Readers' Dictionary
(large print edition)
Young Readers' Thesaurus
(large print edition)

For further information or a free brochure, please contact us at:
Ulverscroft Large Print Books Ltd.,
The Green, Bradgate Road, Anstey,
Leicester, LE7 7FU, England.
Tel: (00 44) **0116 236 4325**
Fax: (00 44) **0116 234 0205**

Other titles in the
Linford Mystery Library:

VICTORIAN VILLAINY

Michael Kurland

Professor James Moriarty stands alone as the particular nemesis of Sherlock Holmes. But just how evil was he? Here are four ingenious stories, all exploring an alternate possibility: that Moriarty wasn't really a villain at all. But why, then, did Holmes describe Moriarty as 'the greatest schemer of all time', and 'the Napoleon of crime'? Holmes could never *catch* Moriarty in any of his imagined schemes — which only reinforced his conviction that the professor was, indeed, an evil genius . . .

THE DYRYSGOL HORROR AND OTHER STORIES

Edmund Glasby

What is the nature of the evil that terrorises Dyrysgol? Detective Inspector Bernard Owen's investigation involves people disappearing from this remote Welsh village. Local anger is directed towards Dyrysgol Castle and its enigmatic owner. But whilst Viscount Ravenwood is a little strange, is he a murderer? Then another man goes missing and his car is left with great claw marks across the roof, as Owen and his officers are dragged towards the bloody conclusion of the mystery of Dyrysgol . . .

WHITE JADE

V. J. Banis

Chris Channing's former fiancé Jeff tells her that his life is in danger: his wife is slowly poisoning him. But is this true? Responding to his claim, Chris goes to him at Morgan House where she's up against the strange brother-in-law David, the cunning wife Mary, and Jeff, the man she'd once loved, but who's now vastly changed. Chris, lost, confused and swept into a powerful undertow of danger, begins to realize that someone is trying to kill her . . .